# RITA, THE WEEKEND RAT

## SONIA LEVITIN

Illustrated by Leonard Shortall

THIS BOOK BELONGS TO
**B.K. ULRICH**

AN
**APPLE**
PAPERBACK

SCHOLASTIC INC.
New York Toronto London Auckland Sydney

*To Danny,*
*Shari, and Lloyd*

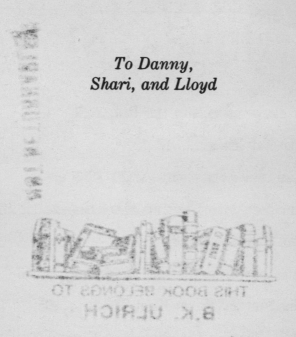

ISBN 0-590-42245-6

Copyright © 1971 by Sonia Levitin. All rights reserved. Published by Scholastic Inc. APPLE PAPERBACKS is a registered trademark of Scholastic Inc.

12 11 10 9 8 7 6 5 4 3 2 1          5          9/8 0 1 2 3 4/9

Printed in the U.S.A.

# Contents

# In Love with Rita the Rat

Cynthia stood by the gate of Mrs. Hanson's kindergarten playground, watching as the children ran out the door. They skipped and hopped and looked so very pleased with themselves that Cynthia was tempted to call out,

> Kindergarten baby,
> Born in the navy!

But Cynthia said nothing, remembering how she used to feel when people teased her about being in kindergarten. Now that she was in fourth grade she looked back at kindergarten with mixed feelings. She would never want to be that little again. But in kindergarten life was very simple.

Cynthia sighed as she watched the last child skip out the gate. Her own life was very complicated. It was mainly Albert's fault. Her brother had just turned eleven. He felt very important, because soon he would move up from Cub Scouts to Boy Scouts. And the more important Albert felt, the bossier he got.

Then there was the matter of the Boys' Club. Cynthia had organized the club, and its three other members, Pete, Benny, and Kevin, were always threatening to throw her out.

"You can't throw me out!" she would say fiercely. "I'm the president!"

"You're a girl," the boys would scoff, until Cynthia replied,

"I'm a tomboy and that's very different." Then she would have to think fast for some project to keep the boys interested, or the club would simply fall apart. And without the Boys' Club, Cynthia would have nothing of her own at all.

Cynthia walked to the door and waited for Mrs. Hanson to notice her.

"Come in, Cynthia!" the teacher said, smiling. "How do you like fourth grade? Have you heard about my new turtle?"

"Fine," Cynthia replied. Then, "No. I came to see Rita."

Mrs. Hanson had bought the white rat last spring. After that, Cynthia had gone to visit Mrs.

2

Hanson at least once a week, so that she could play with Rita. Then came summer vacation, and Cynthia hadn't seen Rita since last June.

"My, Rita's grown," Cynthia said, walking toward the cage which stood on a low shelf.

"Would you like to take her out of the cage?" Mrs. Hanson asked.

"Oh, yes!" Cynthia exclaimed, opening the cage door.

Rita dodged quickly under her treadmill.

"Be careful," Mrs. Hanson warned. "She still bites. I haven't been able to teach that rat any manners all summer."

"Rita never bites me," Cynthia said, adding softly, "She knows I love her."

Rita stared fixedly at Cynthia and twitched her long white whiskers.

"Come on, little darling," Cynthia coaxed. In a flash she caught the rat firmly around the middle and brought her out.

"There, there," Cynthia soothed, holding Rita over her shoulder like a baby. The soft white fur tickled Cynthia's cheek. "I've missed you," she crooned. "Did you have a nice summer?"

"Oh, great," Mrs. Hanson groaned. "She and my cat spent the whole summer fighting. I'll never take that rat to my house again. Never. My poor cat almost had a fit."

"Poor Rita," Cynthia murmured. "No wonder

she bites. It must have been awful for her to live with a cat all summer." It seemed unfair to put the blame on Rita, Cynthia thought. After all, Rita had been helpless in a cage, and that cat was probably a big bully.

Cynthia stroked Rita's head, then gave her a quick kiss. She held the rat up to study her closely. The little pink mouth seemed to tremble, and the tail stuck straight out in fright.

"It seems to me," said Cynthia, "that Rita is on-the-verge-of-a-nervous-breakdown."

Cynthia wasn't exactly sure what that meant, but she thought it was something like a cold, except that it was caused from hearing too much noise. Mrs. Aimsley next door got it often, espe-

cially when Cynthia and the other members of the Boys' Club played wall ball. Mrs. Aimsley's garage door was the best place in the whole neighborhood for playing wall ball.

Mrs. Aimsley would lean out the window and shout, "Stop that banging, Cynthia! I'm on-the-verge-of-a-nervous-breakdown!" Then Mrs. Aimsley would sniff and dab at her nose, which was always a bit red.

"Yes," said Cynthia, noticing that Rita's nose was also quite red. "I think she is on the verge."

"I wouldn't know about that," said Mrs. Hanson. "But a change might do Rita good. I don't know what to do with her on weekends. None of the kindergartners this year wants to take her home."

"I'd love to take her home with me," Cynthia said instantly.

"You would?" The teacher's face brightened. "Really?"

"Sure," Cynthia nodded.

"Would it be all right with your mother?" Mrs. Hanson sounded doubtful.

"My mother loves rats," Cynthia said firmly.

"Then maybe you could take her home every weekend," Mrs. Hanson offered.

Joy, pure joy, filled Cynthia, and with effort she kept her lips from grinning. Happiness, if she let it all come through, would lift her up like a hundred balloons, and she would float out of sight forever!

"Tomorrow's Friday," Mrs. Hanson remembered. "You come and get Rita after school—if it's all right with your parents."

The sidewalk seemed to roll away under Cynthia's feet as she ran the four blocks home. She burst in the door. "Mother! Rita's coming!"

She skidded to a stop at the kitchen table, and her mother caught the milk bottle as it toppled, ready to crash to the floor.

"Cynthia! You scared me out of ten years' growth!"

Cynthia took a quick gulp of milk. "Rita's coming. Tomorrow. All weekend."

"Wait a minute!" Mother sank into a chair. "Don't you ask permission before you invite people to spend the night? Who's Rita, anyway?"

"Don't you remember?" Cynthia frowned. "You never listen to me. She's still in Mrs. Hanson's kindergarten—from last year—she..."

"Poor thing," Mother murmured. "How come she failed kindergarten?"

"Mother!" Cynthia moaned. "You *never* listen to me. Rita didn't flunk. She belongs to Mrs. Hanson. She's a white rat in a cage."

"Oh," Mother grinned. "No wonder she didn't make first grade."

"Can I bring her home? Oh, you'll love her," Cynthia said happily. "She's got the cutest little treadmill and a little water bottle. She's very

6

quiet. You won't even know she's here. In fact, she needs a rest, because she's on-the-verge..."

"Wait a minute!" Mother held her hand up like a traffic policeman. "We'll have to ask your father."

"She's very polite," Cynthia went on. "And she's very clean. She washes her paws before she eats."

"More than I can say for some people," Mother remarked.

"She'll be a playmate for Bruno," Cynthia continued.

"I'm not sure that a rat is a proper playmate for a German shepherd," Mother said.

"You don't want Rita, do you?" Cynthia stared at her mother. "Albert's got Bruno, and you don't even want me to have a weekend rat."

"We'll have to ask your father," her mother said gently. "Of course I want you to have a weekend rat. It—it just never occurred to me before, that's all. It's just a little unexpected."

"*Do* you love animals?" Cynthia demanded.

"Of course I do," her mother declared. "Still, we have to ask your father. Now go change your clothes. I've laid out your pink shorts and top."

"I'll wear that tomorrow," Cynthia called back from the stairs.

"It's always tomorrow." Mother sighed. "Sometimes I wonder why I bother to buy you clothes at all. You're always wearing Albert's."

"The president of the Boys' Club," Cynthia ex-

7

plained patiently, "cannot go around in girls' clothes. Girls are not allowed in the club."

"I see," said her mother.

But her mother never really seemed to understand. It had taken many months of coaxing before her mother had bought her a pair of boys' jeans. With her own money Cynthia had bought herself some boys' black socks at the dime store. Now she put on her jeans and the socks, then crept into Albert's room to rummage through his drawers. She selected his old baseball shirt from Little League. It hung down nearly to her knees, and the neck opening sagged low around her chest. Across the front in white letters were the words CALLOWAY CONSTRUCTION.

In front of the bathroom mirror, Cynthia wet her hair and brushed it down flat. Finally she put on Albert's old blue baseball cap, the visor reaching low over her forehead.

Now, unless she smiled, Cynthia thought with satisfaction, anybody would think she was a boy. As her grandmother often said, "Cynthia's more of a boy than *any* boy," and although that didn't seem to make much sense, Cynthia liked the sound of it. Boys had all the fun in this world. And since last summer, when Cynthia had openly declared herself to be a tomboy, she had decided to take some of that fun for herself.

Why then, she asked herself, were things still so

complicated? Why was Albert bossier than ever? And why had Pete threatened just this morning to quit the club completely?

But all that would change, she decided, scampering down the stairs. Once she owned a weekend rat, there was no end to the things she could do. Rita would be the club mascot. They could put on animal shows! Other boys would want to join, just for a chance to play with Rita.

She ran across the street to Kevin's house, bursting with her news. Kevin's mother had just finished cutting his hair. It was light blond and stood out like a bristle brush. Cynthia gazed at it enviously and asked Kevin's mother, "Would you like to cut my hair?"

"I wouldn't dare," Kevin's mother replied. "I don't think your mother wants you to have a crew cut."

Cynthia sighed. Then, remembering, she announced, "I'm getting a rat. She'll be our club mascot. Aren't you glad you're a member now?"

"Cool," replied Kevin. He was a person of few words.

Pete was waiting for them outside to play wall ball. When he heard about Rita, Pete's freckled face creased into a smile. Then abruptly he frowned and raked his fingers through his red hair.

"Naw," he said. "I bet your dad won't let you keep that rat. They stink, you know."

"Not very much!" Cynthia objected.

"Dads don't like *any* stink," Pete insisted. "He won't want that rat, even for weekends. You'll see."

"Yes he will!" Cynthia stamped her foot angrily, but inside she felt weighed down with doubts. It would all depend on the stock market. That was just one more thing that made Cynthia's life complicated. When the market was up, Daddy was happy. In his happiness he was likely to say "yes" to almost anything. But when it was down—watch out. No wonder Daddy was tired at night, going up and down with that market all day like a yo-yo.

Even before he was in the door, Cynthia ran to Daddy asking, "Is the market up today? Is it?"

Daddy smiled. "Well, a little."

So far so good, thought Cynthia. But how to explain it all so that Daddy would agree to letting a rat share his home every weekend?

"I'm in love, Daddy," she began, hugging his arm. "I'm in love with a rat."

"No good can come of it," Daddy replied. "Try to forget him. Fall in love with a nice kid, like Kevin."

"Not a boy," Cynthia giggled. "A rat in a cage, the cutest white rat you ever saw...."

"Molly, is dinner ready?" Daddy called out to the kitchen.

"In a minute, dear," Mother answered.

"Mrs. Hanson says I can take her home every weekend," Cynthia continued, following Daddy.

"Who?" Daddy took off his shoes and put on his slippers.

"Rita, the rat. The one I love. May I?" Cynthia closed her eyes, crossed her fingers and wished with all her might.

Now Daddy looked at her fully. "You say you love this rat?" he questioned.

Cynthia nodded. "I do."

"Far be it from me to stand in the way of true love," Daddy said in a deep voice. "Get the rat. Now let me eat."

"Were you listening to her, Charles?" Mother asked. "Did you understand? Cynthia wants to bring a rat home every weekend."

"Yes, I understand perfectly," said Daddy. "Most people try to get rid of rats. Your daughter happens to love them. So we'll have a weekend rat. Now, let's have dinner," he said with a nod to indicate that everything was settled.

## The Rat Race

Even Albert was pleased about the idea of having a rat in the house. He wasn't the least bit grouchy, until after dinner when Daddy tried once again to show him how to tie knots. It was the one thing Albert could not seem to learn, and in order to move up from Cubs into Boy Scouts, he had to know the knots.

Daddy strained to be patient, and Albert tried hard to pay attention. But the more he worked with the rope, trying to make a bowline, the more grouchy he became, until finally he flung down the rope in disgust, shouting, "Who needs to tie knots anyway? I'm not going to be a sailor! I'm never going to go mountain climbing. I don't plan to tie a mule to a post...."

"That's enough, son," Daddy warned, and Cynthia picked up the rope, turning it this way and that.

"It's simple," she said under her breath. "All you have to do is..."

Albert snatched the rope away angrily. "What do you know about it? And what are you doing with my shirt? You have no right to sneak into my room when I'm gone. You have no right to wear my clothes. *Mother!*"

Cynthia started to tear after him, but Daddy held her back. "Leave him alone, Cynthia," he said gently. "He's just worried that he won't learn it in time for the investiture. It's less than two months away. Poor Albert. He can't seem to get the hang of it."

"I can do it," Cynthia said.

"Sure you can, honey." Daddy patted her shoulder absent-mindedly, and Cynthia went upstairs wondering dismally why nobody ever really listened to her.

At least the members of the Boys' Club listened to her—when she could get them together. From now on, she decided, they would meet regularly every Friday, when Rita could be present.

During recess at school the next day, Cynthia rounded up Pete, Benny, and Kevin. She motioned them to a quiet place at the side of the building, knowing she had to talk fast, because at school the boys didn't like to be seen with her.

"We're having a club meeting today," she said excitedly, "with our new mascot, Rita the rat."

"I'm not sure I can come," Benny objected. His eyes looked very large and round through his glasses.

"You'd better," Cynthia warned, with a firm, tough look.

"My mom won't let me dig anymore," Benny explained. He rubbed his thumb over his glasses to clean them. He usually had a hard time seeing through the thumb prints, which made him rub still more.

"We won't have to dig anymore," Cynthia assured him. "We'll get a new project." The underground clubhouse she had planned was not going very well. After several weeks of heavy digging, it was no more than a soggy hole in the ground under the walnut tree out back.

"We'll have special events," Cynthia declared. "Meet me in front of Mrs. Hanson's room after school. You can all take turns carrying Rita in the cage."

"You'd better plan something good," Pete said, glancing at a group of boys who were pointing and laughing.

"I have to go now," Benny said quickly. "Joe Tomkins is waiting for me." And Joe Tomkins was standing at the drinking fountain, his cheeks puffed out with water, getting ready to squirt somebody. Joe Tomkins was always doing things like that.

"Me too," said Kevin, rushing off. Cynthia wandered around the playground alone, wondering what kind of special event she could plan.

When the last bell rang, Cynthia still hadn't thought of anything, but as she dashed over to Mrs. Hanson's room it didn't seem to matter. Benny, Pete, and Kevin were waiting excitedly, each begging for the first turn to carry Rita. It would be enough, Cynthia decided, just to have Rita.

As they walked down the street, other children stopped to stare, and Benny sang loudly, "Rat parade! Join the rat parade!"

Little girls with their doll carriages fell into line. Several older boys with baseball bats tagged along, and even the paper boy rode alongside on his bike. But when they passed a group of girls in Girl Scout uniforms, there was only a strange silence. The girls were walking together, arms linked. Betty Filbert, who sat behind Cynthia in class, was with them.

Betty had recently joined the Girl Scouts. Her older sister was a member, too. Sissy stuff, Cynthia called it to herself. But as she walked past the girls she became uncomfortable, wondering what they might be thinking. Perhaps they were thinking, "Lucky Cynthia—she's got a rat and a club and she's having all the fun." But maybe they were thinking something quite different.

Cynthia looked straight ahead. Then Betty

waved and called out, "Hi, Cynthia!" Cynthia waved back. She was tempted to ask Betty to come along, but if the boys ever saw her playing with Betty Filbert they would tease and taunt her, "I thought you were a tomboy! How come you're playing with girls?"

When they arrived at Cynthia's house, Mother threw up her hands, exclaiming, "Cynthia, you look like the Pied Piper! What are all these children doing here?"

"They've come to see Rita," Cynthia explained. Then she faced the noisy group, hands on her hips, and shouted, "Quiet! This rat is on-the-verge-of-a-nervous-breakdown!"

"I will be too," said Mother, "if those children don't quiet down."

"If they had some cookies to eat," Cynthia suggested, "they wouldn't make so much noise. They'd be busy eating."

"Quite so," Mother agreed, shaking her head. "This rat," she mumbled, "is going to mean a lot of work for me."

One at a time Cynthia allowed the children to come forward and gaze at Rita. Soon everyone had a turn, even Kevin's little sister Sara, who was only three. Of course, they were not allowed to touch Rita. That was for club members only.

When only club members remained, Cynthia

took Rita down to the rumpus room and set the cage squarely in the middle of the table. But the cage on the table looked terribly bare. Cynthia ran upstairs, brought back a large white tablecloth and spread it out on the table. Rita crouched down low, looking frightened. Perched there on the white tablecloth, it rather looked as if someone planned to serve her for supper.

"Don't worry, Rita," Cynthia murmured. "I won't let anyone hurt you."

While Pete, Kevin, and Benny took turns holding Rita, Cynthia beamed. "Isn't she beautiful?" she whispered. "Isn't she sweet?"

"You said special events," Pete grumbled. "What fun is it just looking at an old rat?"

"Yeah," added Kevin. "We want to do something."

"Let's go to my house and play wall ball," Benny suggested. "Oh, no," he shook his head. "I forgot. We can't. We just had the house painted."

"Let's go on up to the creek," Pete urged. The boys began to whisper together, and Cynthia felt a moment of panic. She was not allowed near the creek.

She wished she had some plan. Plan ahead, Daddy always said. He even had a sign about it on his desk, PLAN AHEAd, but someone hadn't planned it very well. There was hardly any space for the "D."

Thinking of Daddy, she suddenly had an idea. "I

know!" she exclaimed. "Let's have a rat race."

"What's that?" Pete asked doubtfully, pushing his fingers through his red hair.

"Don't you know?" Cynthia asked in amazement. "Doesn't your dad talk about it? Mine does all the time."

Cynthia sometimes wondered, when Daddy came home muttering, "A regular rat race..." exactly what was going on downtown at his office. She could just about picture it now.

"We'll take turns racing against Rita," she told the boys. "The winner," she smiled, "gets a piece of candy."

"What if the rat wins?" Pete asked suspiciously.

"Cheese for Rita," Cynthia said promptly.

"Where's the candy?" Pete demanded.

"I've got lots of candy," Cynthia assured him. She had saved nearly half her bag of Halloween candy from last year. It was hidden high on her closet shelf behind the stuffed animals. She ran to get it.

"Kevin's first," Cynthia said, "because he's vice-president. All in favor? You have to say EYE," she explained. "That's what they do in my mother's club."

"EYE!" shouted the boys, and Cynthia reached inside the cage. Rita clung to the bars with all four paws, but at last Cynthia pried her loose. She placed the rat on the floor beside Kevin.

Cynthia stepped back and began the count

down. "Ten, nine, eight, seven..." Then she shouted "Go!" and gave Rita a slight push.

The rat darted across the floor, up over the bookcase and down again. Then, with a flying leap, she landed right in the bag of Halloween candy.

"Look! Look!" Benny squealed, holding his sides with laughter. "The rat's in the bag! Look at it shake!" He laughed until his glasses were steamy, and the other boys thumped him on the back, laughing and shouting.

Cynthia tore open the bag to let Rita out. The rat darted away between her outstretched hands. Suddenly Pete gasped and pointed to the doorway, and they all turned to follow his warning finger.

There stood Bruno, his huge black body tense, his head cocked to one side. He moved a step closer, his nose working rapidly. Low in his throat there was a steady rumble, growing louder and more threatening as he approached Rita, who sat shivering in the corner, unable to hide.

## Bad News Saturday

"Bruno!" Cynthia pulled at his collar with one hand, but all one hundred and twenty pounds of Bruno pushed past her. Cynthia pushed with all her might against Bruno, trying at the same time to grasp Rita. Do dogs eat rats? she wondered wildly. If Bruno swallowed Rita, would it kill Rita, or would she swim forever in his tummy?

"Wait!" Pete shouted. "He *likes* her."

Cynthia eased away and saw that the dog was sniffing cautiously, twitching his huge black nose, turning his head from side to side.

"It's Rita," Cynthia whispered to Bruno. "Good dog, Bruno," she said hopefully, "gentle dog."

Bruno raised one paw and held it inches above

Rita's trembling little body. He stepped back, raised his paw again.

"He's trying to shake hands with her," Benny whispered in awe.

Rita settled herself back further against the wall. Bruno stretched out his neck, black nose working frantically. Suddenly Rita struck out with her tiny paw and scratched Bruno right on his tender nose. With a little yelp of complete surprise, Bruno sprang back. He eyed Rita from a distance and Rita's little red eyes gleamed in a firm, fixed stare. She would defend herself, her look seemed to say, and she meant business!

Cynthia watched, scarcely breathing, as Bruno again approached Rita. He moved ever so slowly, gently sniffing, and finally he lay down facing Rita, head on his paws, ears perked up. As always when he was about to rest, Bruno gave a little grunt of satisfaction.

"They're friends now," Cynthia whispered. Gently she replaced Rita in the cage. "The race is over," she told the boys. "Rita's tired."

"Where's Kevin's prize?" Pete demanded. "That was no fair. The rat didn't run right."

"Since Rita didn't finish the race," Cynthia said, "Kevin gets the prize." She reached into the bag and pulled out a Tootsie Roll.

Kevin unwrapped the candy while the other boys watched enviously. Kevin took a bite. He made a strange face. He tried to pull his mouth open.

"Sh-shay," he managed at last. "How old ish thish candy?"

"It's not old," Cynthia objected. "I just got it last Halloween."

"That's nearly a year ago!" Pete exclaimed.

"So what?" Cynthia demanded. "That just makes it better."

"It'sh not bad," said Kevin, swallowing hard. "I guesh I better go home." He picked at his teeth with his fingers.

"Meeting adjourned," Cynthia said hastily, as the boys turned to leave. "Don't forget to come next Friday."

"You promised special events," Pete called back. "It better be good. You better teach that rat to run right."

"I will," Cynthia promised, though she hadn't the slightest idea how this could be accomplished.

Outside the wind was blowing the branches of the pine tree against the window pane with a low, steady thump, thump, thump. It was only seven-thirty, but dark as midnight, and a distant owl was calling faintly, "Who? Who? Who?" as if she, too, wondered who was stealing summer away.

"The nights are getting cold," Daddy remarked, looking up from his newspaper. "Soon we'll have to take the patio furniture and the Ping-Pong table indoors. I don't want to get caught by the rains again this year."

"You can't fit *anything* into that garage," Mother said, shaking her head. "It's filled with junk and old newspapers. Your son," she said, "was supposed to tie up those papers so we could get rid of them."

"*Your* son," Daddy replied, chuckling, "was supposed to get his old pup tent out of there. And your daughter has cartons full of rocks."

"That's my collection," Cynthia said.

"We've got to get things in order," Daddy repeated, "before the rains come. Tomorrow is ..."

Suddenly Mother sniffed at the air. "What's that funny smell?" she asked, turning her head this way and that. She moved closer toward the table. "My white tablecloth!" she cried, snatching it away. She sniffed again. "That," she said accusingly, pointing at Rita, "is the smell. Young lady, you've got to clean that cage in the morning."

"...Saturday," Daddy said, as if he had not been interrupted. "And that means chores."

"That means bad news," Mother put in. "Saturdays," she often said, "are bad news." She gave several reasons for this. Included were people eating cookies and making a mess, people not wiping their feet and making a muddy mess, people bringing in a gang of friends and making a horrible mess.

But the real bad news about Saturdays was that it was garbage day. And if there was one thing Bruno hated, it was seeing those strange men taking away his garbage. It made him furious.

On Saturdays, while Albert and Cynthia cleaned the garage (at least, they were supposed to clean it), Bruno was kept in the back yard. That was a strict rule. For all his power and huge teeth, Bruno was usually as gentle as a lamb, as Mother always told visitors. But as soon as Bruno heard the garbage truck rattling down the street, his gentle nature changed completely. He became, like his ancient ancestors, as wild as a prowling wolf.

His fur would bristle. His lips would curl back in a sneer, showing long and pointed teeth. As the truck stopped in front of the house, Bruno would hurl himself at the gate, barking, banging, warning neighbors for blocks around that *those criminals* were here again.

The fact that nobody seemed to care only made him angrier.

But this Saturday, when Cynthia and Albert were ready to clean Rita's cage, the garbage truck was nowhere in sight. They had made a deal. Albert was going to help Cynthia with Rita, and she was going to help him bundle up the newspapers. The whole thing was to be done in the garage.

"You can hold Rita," Cynthia told Albert, "while I clean the cage."

Albert sat down on top of the freezer with Rita on his head. He looked very strange with Rita's long pink tail curled down around his ear.

Cynthia had watched Mrs. Hanson clean the cage many times. She knew exactly what to do. She unfastened the little hooks on the side and slid out the pan underneath. She cleaned out the small bits of sawdust that clung to the bars. As she worked, an idea began to take shape in her mind.

If she and Albert could clean out the garage completely, get rid of the junk, the old newspapers and magazines that had been accumulating longer than anyone could remember—then Daddy could bring in the patio furniture. And with the furniture all arranged like a room, what a wonderful clubhouse she would have! Cynthia imagined it clearly, holding her club meetings there, while outside it was cold and wet. It wouldn't matter. Safe and warm in the clubhouse, she and the boys would make wonderful projects at the large wooden picnic table. Banners and signs would decorate the walls — KEEP OUT. NO GURLS ALOUD.

Excitedly she told Albert her idea. "You'd freeze," Albert said scornfully. "There's no heat out here."

"We could use the little electric heater," Cynthia said.

"You'd never get it clean enough. You always

start things," Albert pointed out, "and you never finish them. You just make a big mess."

"That's not true!" Cynthia cried tearfully, but to herself she had to admit that it was. The hole in the back yard was just one example of a project she had begun and never finished.

She sighed deeply. She'd show Albert. She'd show everyone! At least she would take proper care of Rita. She gathered up the soiled paper, spread a fresh piece on the bottom and covered it with sawdust.

"You hold onto Rita," she told Albert. "I'm going to put this old paper in the incinerator."

Albert lay down on his back with the rat still on his head. "Hurry up," he said crossly. "I haven't got all day."

Cynthia went around into the yard and put the paper in the incinerator. She was doing everything exactly right, she thought, smiling to herself. Suddenly everything went wrong.

Cynthia, engrossed in her work, had not heard the garbage truck come rattling down the street. She had not seen Bruno streak past her when she opened the gate. She had, in fact, done nothing wrong at all. But the sounds she heard coming from the garage were like nothing short of a full-scale battle.

She ran toward the confusion of sounds, the crashing, clanging, shouting, barking. Bruno had waited behind a bush, letting the garbage man approach. He had let the man pick up the garbage can, waiting to catch him in the act of theft. And then Bruno had closed in.

Thus Cynthia arrived on the scene just as the terrified garbage man sent the can crashing down onto the concrete floor. The can rolled down the driveway, sending its contents flying this way and that, while Bruno held the man locked against the wall.

Bruno's tail stuck straight out. The fur on his back rose up to a dangerous peak, and his powerful jaws came together with a snap! snap! snap! while deep in Bruno's throat came the low rumble of attack.

The man rolled his eyes sideways. He caught up an old chair and thrust it out in front of himself like a lion tamer facing a vicious cat.

"Haw! Haw!" roared the man, jabbing the chair at Bruno. "Back! Back!"

And Bruno leaped wildly higher and higher.

"Bruno!" screamed Cynthia. "Sit!"

It was the only command Bruno knew, but he wasn't listening.

"He's gentle as a lamb," Cynthia shouted to the garbage man, but he wasn't listening either.

Cynthia whirled around for an instant and saw a white blur as Rita jumped down from Albert's head and dashed behind the freezer while Albert ran for the garden hose.

If there was one thing that Bruno hated even more than criminals stealing his garbage, it was water.

Cynthia grasped Bruno's collar and was nearly pulled flat on her face. Then she felt the rush of cold water over her head.

All at once Daddy was there, with Mother close behind him, and the dripping, humiliated dog was dragged away. The garbage man, still holding the chair, looked dazed as he mopped his head with a large handkerchief. He, too, was dripping wet.

"Are you hurt?" Mother asked anxiously.

The man put down the chair. "That dog," he said, still panting, "should be sent to the U.S. Army. They're always looking for fighters."

"I don't know what got into him," Mother frowned, wringing her hands. "He's usually gentle as a lamb."

"Lady," said the garbage man, "you and me must be talking about two different dogs."

While Mother apologized, Cynthia surveyed the mess. The garage floor was thick with soggy newspaper and garbage. She shivered and put her hand to her head and pulled a piece of orange peel from her hair. Then she remembered Rita.

"Rita's behind the freezer!" she cried.

"Who's Rita?" asked the man, backing away.

"Just a rat," Mother explained.

The garbage man backed away toward his truck.

He rushed inside, slammed the door and was off, muttering to himself.

"Oh-oh," Daddy said with a strange look. Then, in a low voice, he spelled out the word P-O-I-S-O-N.

"Help me move the freezer, quickly," he murmured to Albert.

"Maybe we'll have to have her stomach pumped," Albert said in a worried tone.

"Whose stomach?" Cynthia cried, and a sudden feeling of fear made her shiver even more than the cold. "Who? What's wrong?" Then she recognized that word, *poison*. She remembered watching the pest control man put little packets of rat poison up in the attic, under the house, and behind the freezer. "They can't resist this stuff," the man had said. "It's quick and sure."

Cynthia ran toward the freezer, tears blurring her eyes. "Rita," she sobbed. "Oh, Rita, come out. Don't eat anything. Oh, Rita!"

## The Rat with Rhythm and a Sneeze

Straining and pulling, Daddy and Albert moved the freezer. "Careful," Albert directed. "We don't want to squash her."

Cynthia watched, motionless from fear.

The freezer moved just a little, then a little more. Cynthia scrambled up on top. Peering down into the dark space she saw Rita's gleaming eyes. She scooted down into the narrow space, snatched up Rita and brought her out.

Again and again she kissed Rita's head and squeezed the rat so tightly that her tail stuck straight out, then snapped back into a curl the shape of the letter S.

"I don't suppose she was back there long enough

to have gotten into the poison," Daddy said. "Probably she was too frightened to eat, anyway. But you'd better give her plenty of water, Cynthia. Last night I noticed that Rita's water bottle was almost empty. If you keep an animal," he said reproachfully, "you've got to take care of it."

"I will, Daddy," Cynthia whispered, thankful that Rita was safe.

Even with Daddy's help it took several hours to restore some kind of order to the garage and to soothe Bruno's feelings. Wet and miserable, he hid outside in the petunia bed, adding a layer of mud and dry leaves to his fur.

Bruno sighed deeply and rolled his eyes at the insult of having to be washed down with pet shampoo, then rinsed off with the hose. When Albert and Cynthia wrapped him in a large bath towel, Bruno lay on his back playing dead, refusing to look either of them in the eye.

At last the garage floor had been swept clean, and the wet papers had been spread out to dry. It would be impossible to tie them up that day, and Albert, hiding a grin, went off to work on his last Cub Scout project.

He was still working on it that night when they all sat in the rumpus room. For the project, called Tools Achievement, Albert had fastened several boards together and was attaching numerous hooks and hinges of different sizes. Cynthia

33

couldn't even guess what it was, and she had no intention of asking.

Cynthia sat on the sofa watching Rita crack sunflower seeds with her teeth. Bruno sat at Daddy's feet, waiting. When Daddy had finished reading the paper, he folded it up again and gave it to Bruno, who ran with it to the door leading to the garage. Bruno waited patiently until Cynthia opened the door. Then he ran and dropped the paper among the pile of other papers.

This was Bruno's daily responsibility, along with fetching the newspaper when it was dropped on the porch each afternoon. Cynthia, remembering how Daddy had trained Bruno, asked suddenly, "Daddy, do rats learn by — by assassination?"

Daddy chuckled. "I hope not."

"*Association*, you nut," Albert said scornfully. "Sure they do. All animals do." He looked up from his hammering to explain. "If you want to train an animal, you wait until he's ready to do the thing you want. When he does it, you say the command, then give him a reward."

"That's right," Daddy said. "Remember the day Bruno picked up the paper? I said 'fetch paper,' and then gave him a dog biscuit. Soon he had learned it."

Cynthia thought hard for a few minutes. She knew what the reward would be — a piece of cheese. But how could she make Rita start running?

"Let's have some music," Daddy suggested, walking to the phonograph.

"Play this one," Cynthia said, taking down her favorite record. It was called "Down Mexico Way," a gay piece with singing trumpets, strumming guitars, and lively snapping drums.

As Daddy started the record, Cynthia's foot began to tap with the rhythm. Albert's hammer followed the beat. Suddenly Daddy called out, "Hey! Look at Rita! That rat's got rhythm."

Excited by the sound of the music, Rita was running round and round on her treadmill. The wheel spun with a clickety-clickety-squeak under Rita's swift little paws. Faster and faster she ran, with ears pressed flat against her head and nose pointed up. Clickety-clickety-*squeak*. Rita's eyes were half closed in an expression of sheer joy.

When the song was over, Rita jumped down from her treadmill and drank greedily from her water bottle.

Cynthia dashed to the kitchen, returning with a piece of cheese. Rita's training had begun.

It was one thing to run on a treadmill, but quite another to run a proper race. For the rest of the evening and long after she had gone to bed, Cynthia puzzled over her problem. What would make Rita run straight? Dimly Cynthia recalled seeing pictures of horse races on television and hearing the announcer's voice, "The horses are at the starting gate ... they're in the track ... "

Of course! Rita needed a track, something with sides on it to keep her running in a straight line. It wouldn't even need a bottom, just sides, like a long thin frame. There was plenty of wood out in the back yard. But she would need help. Albert.

The next day she approached Albert as he was working on his oddly shaped wooden thing.

"That looks very interesting," she began. "I guess it is very useful."

"Don't know," Albert said, frowning over his work. "I'm just experimenting."

"I guess when you're older," Cynthia continued, "you'll make real good things out of wood—maybe even things for me."

Albert didn't answer.

"Like now," Cynthia went on casually, "I need a track so Rita will run straight."

"Why should she run straight?" Albert asked.

"It's club business," Cynthia told him. After a pause she said, "I guess you wouldn't know how to make a track yet. You'd sure have to know a lot about tools. Maybe Max Martins could do it. He's an *Eagle Scout.*"

Albert brought down the hammer so hard that his board jumped back up. "Max Martins!" he shouted. "Max Martins! What's so great about Max Martins? Anybody can put pieces of wood together. Anybody could make a track for a rat."

"It would count for your Tools Achievement,"

Cynthia added quickly, handing Albert his Scout Book. It was true, for the book said, "Make a useful household object or a game out of wood."

Thus Albert set to work, and Cynthia stood beside him, ready to hand him the tools, to drag long boards into the garage, to marvel, and to compliment his skill.

Cynthia measured Rita across the stomach with a tape measure. The track had to be just wide enough to fit her little body, so that she wouldn't turn around and run the wrong way.

At last the track was finished, and for the rest of the afternoon the rumpus room was the scene of a spirited rat race. Cynthia placed a piece of cheese at the end of the track. Then she started the music. At the same time Albert let go of Rita and they both shouted, "Run!"

For the following two Fridays the members of the Boys' Club were delighted with the rat race. Rita always won, and Mother was puzzled and amazed, saying, "I've never seen this family eat so much *cheese*!" Although Rita won, Cynthia always gave a candy prize for second place, until too soon all the candy was gone and the boys began to grumble.

"What fun is a race without prizes?" Pete said.

"A club ought to be exciting," Benny agreed. "Joe Tomkins says a club should have carnivals and picnics and real neat plans."

"Yeah," said Kevin.

"Joe Tomkins says maybe he's gonna start his own club," Benny announced.

"Really?" Pete looked very interested. "Who will be in it?"

"You can be in it, I guess," Benny said.

Cynthia's heart sank. If Joe Tomkins did start a club, she would be completely left out. Joe Tomkins wouldn't have anything to do with girls, even if they were tomboys. He had four older sisters, and his feelings about girls were no secret.

"Meeting come to order!" Cynthia shouted, stalling for time. Clearly, something had to be done, and fast. She stood up very straight and pulled her baseball cap down over her forehead.

"What we need," she declared, "is a treasurer. Pete, you're the oldest. You should be treasurer. When we get some money we'll be able to do things, big things like — like having a carnival. You'll have to take charge of all that money," she said. "It's a very important job. All in favor for Pete to be treasurer, say Eye."

"Eye!" said the boys in a chorus.

Pete squared his shoulders, looking very proud. Then he turned to Cynthia, frowning. "How can we have a treasurer if we don't have any money?"

"We'll all pay dues," Cynthia decided. "And we'll think of ways to raise money. We'll talk about that next week. Rita is very sleepy. Meeting adjourned."

Rita was, indeed, very sleepy. She lay curled up in a ball, her head resting on her feeding dish. Cynthia could not resist picking her up. She held the sleepy little rat tenderly against her chest, stroking the soft fur with her finger tip.

The little body was soft and warm. Each tiny paw was perfect. The pink eyes were so very bright, the tail so long and firm. Cynthia sighed contentedly.

"I love you, Rita," she whispered. "You're a weekend rat, did you know that? I wish you were mine forever. I hope you live to be at least fifty years old." Cynthia could imagine herself, grown and married, with children of her own, still going

every Friday to Mrs. Hanson's room to take Rita home for the weekend.

Of course she herself would have changed by then, Cynthia thought. "You won't want to be a tomboy when you get older," Mother sometimes told her. "You'll be satisfied just to be yourself."

"I *am* myself," Cynthia would object heatedly. "I just don't like that sissy stuff!"

As she lay in her bed that night, half asleep, Cynthia felt happy and secure. That Joe Tomkins couldn't scare her with his talk about starting a club. Nobody could scare her. She was president of the Boys' Club, and she had a weekend rat. Life was good.

Cynthia knew exactly when the worry began, although she didn't confess it to anyone. It was on Sunday night. She and Albert had spent the afternoon happily racing against Rita. That night, just when the news came on, Rita woke up.

The brisk march music announcing the program made her ears perk up. With a leap she was on her treadmill, running round and round, and the wheel went clickety-clickety-*squeak*.

"Oil!" Daddy shouted. "I can't hear a thing."

Still Rita ran.

"Keep that rat quiet! Can't you oil that wheel? Oh," Daddy groaned. "Now I've missed the football scores."

Just when the program was nearly over Rita jumped off the treadmill and sat down under it.

"Ah," Daddy sighed with relief. "Hush, now." He strained to listen for the business news, and just as the announcer said "stock market," Rita began to sniff and sneeze.

"That rat!" Daddy complained. "Get that rat a handkerchief."

Sniff. Snuff. Sneeze.

"Now I've missed it," Daddy said sorrowfully.

"It's only for weekends, Charles," Mother said quickly. "The rat is usually pretty quiet. She probably just got some dust in her nose."

But the following weekend it was the same thing all over again. Just when they were all settled in the rumpus room, Rita began to sniff and sneeze most violently. And for Cynthia the worry turned into a fear that she could almost taste and feel. Daddy would not let her bring Rita home anymore. Or, worse, Rita was sick.

Late that night, unable to sleep, Cynthia came downstairs to assure herself that Rita was all right.

"What are you doing up?" Mother asked, startled.

"I wanted to say good night to Rita again," Cynthia murmured.

"Well, come on. I'm just going down to take her a crust of bread. You know, you haven't been filling her feeding dish every day, Cynthia. It's really your responsibility."

Cynthia's cheeks flushed with the knowledge

that it was so. Often she forgot about feeding Rita, and in the back of her mind she knew that her mother would tend to it.

Cynthia followed her mother down the stairs. Mother's high-heeled slippers made sharp little clomping sounds.

Suddenly Mother stopped and pointed to the cage. "Look at that!" she exclaimed. "Rita's standing up at the door of her cage. I think she *knew* I was coming to feed her."

"How could she know?" Cynthia asked.

"I usually feed her some scraps at night," Mother explained. "I'm always wearing these slippers, and they make a noise on the stairs. Do you suppose that Rita has learned that the sound of my slippers means food?"

"She is a very smart rat," Cynthia replied, smiling. "Let's try it again."

They went to get more bread, and again Rita scurried to the door of her cage at the sound of Mother's slippers on the stairs.

"You've taught her a trick!" Cynthia hugged her mother tightly.

Rita, having finished the bread, began to sniff and sneeze.

"You do like Rita, don't you?" Cynthia asked her mother pleadingly.

"Of course I do. Perhaps I don't love her quite the way you do, but — yes, I like her," Mother admitted.

"If — if anything happened to her," Cynthia began, "would you be sad?"

Mother put her hand on Cynthia's cheek. "Cynthia," she said seriously, "are you worried about that sneezing? Is that why you can't sleep?"

Cynthia nodded.

"It's probably nothing," Mother said. "But still, perhaps you ought to ask Mrs. Hanson about it. If Rita is sick ... "

"She's not, she's *not!*" Cynthia cried, and she ran upstairs to press her face into her pillow.

# The Disaster Knot

When Cynthia returned Rita to Mrs. Hanson the next day, the teacher promised to watch the rat closely all that week. Perhaps there was nothing wrong with Rita at all.

October had begun, leaving Indian summer days far behind. The sun still shone to clear away the early morning mist, but its rays had lost their summer strength. By Halloween, Cynthia knew, the mornings would be cold and frosty. Front lawns would be covered with a thin sparkling blanket of half-frozen dew.

October, it seemed, made everybody hurry. Mother rushed to club meetings, Daddy rushed off to work, and Albert worked over his Scout book with frantic determination. The Boy Scout investiture was to be held on the last day of the month, Halloween Saturday.

If Cynthia came to the door of his bedroom, Albert would shout crossly, "Go away! Get out of my room!" Then he would return to his book, trying to memorize all the parts of the Scout Oath and the Scout Law. Or he would gaze longingly at the picture of the Scout uniform. They would buy it, Daddy had said, after Albert learned all the knots —the square knot, the bowline, the half-hitch, the sheet bend, and all the others.

Max Martins, the Eagle Scout down the street, tried to teach Albert. At last he gave up, shaking his head.

"You're hopeless, Albert," he said. "Maybe there's something wrong with your fingers."

"There's nothing wrong with my fingers," Albert retorted sharply. "It's just that my head doesn't understand what my fingers are doing."

"You've got to *concentrate*," Daddy said, as he helped Albert in the evening. "It's not really difficult."

Cynthia sat watching them, keeping absolutely silent.

At last Daddy told Albert, "That's enough for tonight, son. We'll try again tomorrow." He picked up his newspaper, and Cynthia quietly picked up the rope that her brother had flung down before he went to his room.

She put the rope around her waist, worked with the short end, then pulled tightly. She had made a perfect bowline. Just then Daddy looked up.

"Cynthia!" he exclaimed. "How did you learn to do that?"

"By watching you and Albert," Cynthia replied, smiling slightly. "It's easy. I can do the others, too."

"It's *not* easy," Daddy protested. "I just told Albert that to encourage him." He leaned forward, watching with great interest. "Do the others," he said, and Cynthia did.

"That's wonderful," Daddy said, giving Cynthia a quick hug. Then he frowned. "You'd better not tell Albert that you've learned these knots. He'd feel terrible."

"I won't," Cynthia nodded, "unless—unless he asks me."


"Rita seems all right to me," said Mrs. Hanson, when Cynthia went to check after school on Wednesday. "She's hardly sneezed at all."

"That's strange," Cynthia mused. "At my house she sneezes all the time, especially when Daddy is watching the news."

"Maybe she doesn't like the program," Mrs. Hanson said lightly. In a serious tone she continued. "It has occurred to me, Cynthia, that maybe all this moving around isn't good for Rita. Rats, you know, are very sensitive to temperature changes. It's getting chilly in the mornings, and you have to keep taking Rita back and forth from school."

Cynthia stared at Mrs. Hanson woodenly. No more Rita on weekends? No more rat race? "It isn't fair!" Cynthia wanted to cry out. "I love Rita." But she said nothing.

"Rita ought to get settled before winter," the teacher continued. "Actually, I don't really need her in my kindergarten room. One of my boys, Stuart Brooks, has a pet rat that he could bring once in a while for the children to play with. So," said Mrs. Hanson with a smile, "Rita could be yours."

Cynthia gasped. "For keeps?" It was too sudden, too wonderful, and happy tears stung at her eyes.

"For keeps," Mrs. Hanson nodded. "You have been very faithful in getting Rita every weekend. And you've given her love. She doesn't even bite anymore."

"Oh, Mrs. Hanson..." Cynthia could not think of the words to express her happiness. "Oh, thank you," she breathed, although the words seemed far too simple.

"I'll give you all the sawdust that's left," Mrs. Hanson continued, "and Rita's food pellets. But you'd better check with your parents. Do you think they'll let you keep Rita?"

"Oh, they love animals," Cynthia said quickly.

"Of course they will. Rita's so sweet. She doesn't bother anyone. ..." And then, abruptly, Cynthia's memory caught up with the words she was saying so eagerly.

Just last weekend she had heard Daddy complaining bitterly. "That rat has taken over completely. I can't even hear the news anymore. She runs and sneezes — honestly, that little thing is noisier than Bruno."

"It's only for weekends, Charles," Mother had soothed.

"Do you think Cynthia really cares about her?" Daddy had protested. "She never cleans the cage anymore. I come down at night and have to fill the water bottle myself. Cynthia isn't really taking responsibility for her pet."

"She loves that rat, Charles," Mother had said gently. "And it's only for weekends. Let's try to put up with it for Cynthia's sake."

"I'll ask them," Cynthia said now in a low, unsteady voice. Having a rat for keeps was a very different thing from having a weekend rat. All that afternoon Cynthia hoped with all her might that the stock market would be up.

She wished so very hard that by five o'clock she felt certain that Daddy would say "Yes." She sped along the street on her bike, feeling the wind in her hair, and when she saw Kevin she called out, "I'm getting Rita for keeps!"

Kevin followed along on his bike, and together they told Pete. "We'll all pay our dues on Friday," Pete said with authority. "Then we'll have money to buy prizes so we can have the rat race again."

The three of them went to tell Benny. "I'll bring a dime on Friday," Benny said firmly. Then he took off his glasses, rubbed them with his thumb, and shook his head sadly. "I forgot," he confessed. "I don't have any money. I don't get any allowance until I pay for the glasses I broke last month."

Cynthia sighed. Losing or breaking his glasses was an old problem for Benny. He never seemed to be able to catch up with his allowance.

But then Benny's face brightened. "I know!" he exclaimed. "My mother will give me a dime for the popsicle man. I'll save that instead of buying a popsicle. I'll pay my dues."

"That's a good idea," Cynthia said, smiling. "The club is more important."

But as she rode off she heard Benny muttering to himself, "But I sure do like popsicles."

Daddy had telephoned to say he would be home late. Cynthia felt that she would explode from trying to be patient. She had said nothing to her mother about Mrs. Hanson's offer. If Daddy gave his permission, she knew her mother would agree.

Listlessly Cynthia went out into the garage, looking for Albert.

She watched as Albert brought a long length of rope across the garage. His tent was spread out on the floor. "What are you doing?" she asked. "Why don't you set it up outside?"

"Don't have any tent stakes," Albert said. "I'll just hang it over this rope."

"Why?" Cynthia asked.

Albert glared at her. "Just because I want to, that's why!"

Albert had fastened one end of the rope to the side door. Now he looped the other end around the shelf on the opposite wall, frowning in concentration as he tied a thick, lumpy knot.

"What kind of a knot is that?" Cynthia asked.

"My own kind," Albert snapped. "Can't a guy invent a knot of his own?"

"You should have a square knot there," Cynthia suggested. "Want me to make one for you?"

"No! Now, look out. You're stepping on the tent. Get out of here." Albert looked down at her feet. "Are those my socks?"

"No!" Cynthia shouted. "They're the ones I bought. I was just going to help you. You're so mean—you're too mean to be a Scout. A Scout is *friendly*," she reminded him heatedly, and before Albert could grab at her, Cynthia fled into the house.

He'll just be a Cub Scout all his life, Cynthia thought angrily. See if I care. I won't teach him the knots, even if he asks me. She did not realize that

she had spoken the last sentence aloud.

"You won't help your brother?" Mother asked, looking up from the stove.

"He won't let me," Cynthia mumbled. "He's so mean and bossy."

"He's unhappy," Mother said gently, "and worried. When you love somebody, you don't punish him for being unhappy. You try to help."

"He thinks I'm a dope," Cynthia murmured.

"Maybe you can think of a way to help him," Mother said, "without making him feel too embarrassed. After all, it's hard for a boy to admit that his younger sister can learn something more easily than he."

"Is Albert stupid?" Cynthia asked.

"No," Mother replied. "He's just nervous. I guess he's trying too hard. It's very important to him to become a Boy Scout."

Without being told, Cynthia began to set the table. "Thank you, Cynthia," Mother said, giving her a warm smile.

Perhaps she should tell Mother first about Rita, Cynthia thought. It wouldn't hurt to have Mother on her side. "Mother," she began. "Mrs. Hanson said that I can ... "

But the sudden sound of screeching tires and the sharp blast of a horn stopped her.

Daddy was home, and his angry voice could be heard clear up in the kitchen. The stock market,

Cynthia thought miserably, must have hit bottom.

All through dinner Cynthia sat quietly, keeping her secret safe, although she felt that surely it must show in her eyes. She would say nothing about it. The time was wrong. The crash in the garage had been a bad beginning. Daddy had come storming into the house. "Something had to give!" he shouted. "That whole darn shelf ripped right out of the wall!"

Little by little they heard the whole story. It was a short story, but grim. Daddy, unsuspecting, had driven his car into the dark garage. Perhaps he had not been paying attention, but *still*, who would expect to find a rope strung up across the garage? Who would expect the rope to be tied to the shelf with a sturdy knot? The rope was so strong that it did not break even when Daddy's car hit it. The knot was so sturdy that it remained in place through the impact.

"Something had to give!" Daddy repeated. The shelf at the side of the garage, to which the rope was tied, ripped right out of the wall. On the shelf was an accumulation of old rubber boots, fishing gear, tin cans filled with old nails, and countless magazines and newspapers. "Everything," said Daddy, "came crashing down."

Daddy turned to Albert. "What kind of a crazy knot was that, anyway? It's all lumpy and strange . . ."

"Let's call it a *disaster knot*," Mother said, hiding a smile behind her hand.

"I'll talk to your son later," Daddy declared.

There was silence through most of the meal, except for polite requests such as, "Please pass the butter." And in the silence Cynthia's mind wandered back over what Mrs. Hanson had said that afternoon. "Rita could be yours — for keeps." So strong was the memory of her happiness then, and so exciting was the secret she had kept all afternoon, that the words suddenly sprang to Cynthia's lips without her even realizing it.

"Did you have a good day, Daddy?"

"A regular rat race," Daddy muttered.

But so intent was Cynthia on her thoughts of Rita, that she hardly heard Daddy's reply, or if she heard, it didn't make any difference.

"I had a wonderful day...." And she began to speak rapidly, eagerly, about Rita and Mrs. Hanson, though all the while a little voice inside her was warning, "It's the wrong time! Not now! Wait!"

Still the words would not stop; they tumbled out like the water of a mountain creek rushing over bright pebbles. "And Rita is so sweet," she heard herself saying. "I want her for my own. I'll take care of her completely. You'll see. I'll even keep her from sneezing. Oh, Daddy, please, may I have Rita for keeps?"

When she had finished Cynthia sat back, her cheeks flushed. Nobody said anything. In the silence Cynthia began to squirm uncomfortably.

Daddy cleared his throat. He gave Cynthia a long, searching look. Then he said, "We'll discuss this later."

For the rest of the meal Daddy remained silent. And that particular kind of silence, from Daddy, was the loudest, longest silence in the world.

While Cynthia helped Mother with the dishes, Daddy called Albert into the living room and closed the door behind them. Whatever passed between Daddy and Albert, Cynthia didn't know. They were together for a long time, without a single sound coming through the walls. When Albert came out his face was solemn and tearful, but he held himself very straight and tall.

"Cynthia!" Daddy called, and it was her turn to stand before her father.

# A Good Bargain's Bad Beginning

"You want to keep Rita," Daddy said earnestly, when Cynthia stood before him. "I don't think you are ready for that kind of responsibility."

"I *am*," Cynthia broke in, but Daddy stopped her with his hand on her shoulder.

"An animal," he said sternly, "is not a toy. It's a living creature. And life," he said, "is very important. It's a serious thing to be responsible for another creature's life — even a rat's," he added softly.

"An animal must be fed regularly," Daddy continued. "It must be kept clean. It must be given water. And most important," Daddy said firmly, "taking care of that animal must not keep you from doing your regular chores."

"I set the table today without being told," Cynthia put in.

"That's fine," said Daddy. "But the table needs to be set *every* day. And that garage," he continued, "needs to be swept *every* week. You and your brother are supposed to work together on that."

"It's hard to work with Albert," Cynthia complained.

"You'll have to find a way to work together," Daddy replied. "I've spoken to Albert about it too. You know, he asked me to let you keep Rita."

"Did he?" Cynthia asked, astonished.

"He did. He knows how much it means to you. Albert is going to try very hard to learn those knots before the investiture. Maybe somehow, *somebody* will find a way to teach him. He has also promised to keep that garage in apple pie order, which includes clearing out all the junk and bundling up all those papers."

"What about Rita?" Cynthia whispered.

"Rita," Daddy repeated gravely, deep in thought. "I'll make a bargan with you, Cynthia. You say you are ready to take complete care of her. I want you to prove it to me. For the next three weekends you bring Rita home just as before. You prove to me that you can take proper care of her without neglecting your other chores. At the end of those three weeks, if you have kept your part of the bargain, Rita will be yours."

"For keeps?" Cynthia breathed.

"For keeps," said Daddy, shaking her hand to seal the bargain. "And let's all hope that she learns to listen respectfully to the evening news." Daddy smiled.

Cynthia ran into her father's arms, and Daddy tousled her hair fondly. "I'll keep my bargain," she said happily. "You'll see."

The next day Cynthia told Mrs. Hanson all about the bargain. On Friday morning Cynthia ran all the way to school. Surely, she thought, skipping up to the playground, this was the very best day of her life. It was the beginning of her bargain, the beginning of club dues, and the beginning of a new project for the club. They would spend only part of their money on candy for rat race prizes. The rest would be saved for something really wonderful, like a club carnival.

It was still early, but Benny was already on the playground. Cynthia ran up to him.

"Hi," she called. "Today's our meeting and we all pay dues. I've got a great idea for a club carni..."

Before she could finish Benny interrupted. "It's gone."

"What?"

"My dime."

"But Benny, you said you'd save your popsicle money."

"I thought I would," Benny explained, looking down at his shoes. "I had it all planned. When I heard the popsicle man's music, I wasn't even going to go outside. I heard the music. I ran out, just to see. I wasn't going to buy anything!"

Benny's voice dropped. "I saw all the other kids buying popsicles, and before I knew it I . . . I just couldn't *stop* myself."

Benny sighed deeply, glancing at Cynthia, and he looked so unhappy that Cynthia felt sorry for him. But suddenly his expression and his tone changed.

"So what?" he demanded. "I have a right to buy a popsicle with my own money."

Out of the corner of her eye Cynthia saw Joe Tomkins walking toward them.

"I'm tired of you telling me what to do and how to spend my money," Benny said loudly. "You're just a *girl*."

Joe Tomkins had caught up with them by now, and Benny repeated, "Just a dumb old girl!"

Cynthia's fists clenched in anger, but she turned on her heels and walked the other way. She was doing exactly as her mother had often told her. "Just turn around and walk away when people make you angry. Don't stay around and fight." But as she walked, Cynthia felt her face getting hotter and hotter, and inside she got angrier and angrier. She was so very angry that she was going to swing all the way across on the big rings without stopping. She'd show them!

She climbed up onto the rings and began to

swing furiously, letting go with one hand, catching hold of the next large ring, moving across like the monkeys at the zoo.

Suddenly there were Benny and Joe Tomkins, laughing and shouting together,

*"I see London*
*I see France*
*I see Cynthia's underpants!"*

Cynthia was so furious that she jumped down in the middle of a swing and skinned her knee. Then she took off after Benny, fists swinging.

"You can't hit me!" Benny cried. "I'm wearing glasses."

And Joe Tomkins yelled, "Let her have it, Benny! Let her have it!"

"You can't hit *me*," Cynthia retorted. "You can't hit a girl."

"Oh! Oh!" Benny cried gleefully, nodding at Joe Tomkins. "You hear that, Joe? She admits she's a girl. Nothing but a girl with underpants showing."

And then Cynthia let Benny have it right in the stomach. Benny's glasses fell off. He doubled over, then flattened out on the ground.

"Get up. Get up, Benny. You're faking," Cynthia shouted, standing over him, and then she felt a heavy hand on her shoulder. It was the yard duty teacher.

"She hit my friend," Joe said, looking wide-eyed and innocent. "He's out cold. She did it. And he was wearing glasses, too."

Cynthia saw Benny open one eye half way. Then quickly he closed it again.

"He's faking," she cried, pointing, but Benny remained motionless. The yard duty teacher took Cynthia by the back of the neck and marched her down the hall, muttering, "Whatever got into you? Why would a nice child like you do such a thing?"

"He called me a girl," Cynthia said heatedly.

"Well..." The yard duty teacher's mouth snapped shut. "Well, we'll see what Miss Klampert has to say about this. Maybe she'll send you to the principal."

Cynthia had never been sent to the principal.

But she had heard about terrible things happening to people who got sent to his office. Very clearly Cynthia recalled every one of those terrible things as they walked to her classroom.

Miss Klampert listened carefully to the yard duty teacher. At last she said sternly, "You will be punished, Cynthia. You will stay after school today for forty-five minutes."

"But Miss Klampert," Cynthia stammered, trying very hard not to cry, "what about Rita? I have to take her home..."

"You'll have to see your friend another time," Miss Klampert snapped. "Now, not another word. Sit down at your desk. And you'll sit on the bench during recess today."

After school, when all the children had left, Cynthia sat in her seat waiting while Miss Klampert corrected papers. At last Miss Klampert looked up and said, "Now, Cynthia, I want you to write, neatly and nicely, 'I will behave like a lady.' Three hundred times."

Cynthia sighed deeply. Then she took several pieces of lined paper from the cupboard and wrote in careful, large letters: NEETLY AND NICLY I WILL BEHAV LIK A LADY.

All the while she was writing, Cynthia pleaded silently, "Don't leave, Mrs. Hanson. Wait for me!"

When she had finished, Cynthia brought the papers to Miss Klampert. Miss Klampert looked at them. Her nose twitched. She peered at Cynthia over her glasses. "Is this what I told you to write?" she demanded.

"Yes, Miss Klampert," Cynthia said meekly. "'Neatly and nicely I will behave like a lady.'"

"Very well, Cynthia," the teacher said, clearing her throat. "You may go now."

"It's probably too late to get Rita," Cynthia mumbled.

"Why don't you phone her when you get home?" Miss Klampert said pleasantly. "I'm really glad you have a little girl friend to play with, instead of running around with those rough boys."

Cynthia only looked at Miss Klampert. What was the use of trying to explain? She ran all the way to the kindergarten building. The gate was open, and Cynthia's heart raced. But when she got to the door it was locked. The room was dark.

Cynthia shook the door, but it wouldn't budge. She felt tears sliding down her cheeks. Then she heard a bike skidding to a stop behind her. It was Joe Tomkins, munching an apple.

"Hi," he said, as if he had forgotten about the fight.

Cynthia didn't answer.

"You looking for Mrs. Hanson?"

Cynthia nodded.

"She's gone home," said Joe, kicking a pebble. He nodded toward the parking lot. "See? Her car's gone. She had a rat with her," he added, and Cynthia rushed toward him.

"Did she? A big white rat? Rita?"

"Dunno the rat's name," Joe said. "But she was getting rid of it. Too much trouble to keep, I guess. She was takin' it to a pet store."

"A pet store?" Cynthia repeated, dazed.

"Yup. I guess if nobody buys it they'll send it to the pound." He gave the pebble another kick. "If nobody claims it they'll send it to a lab. If they send it to a lab," Joe said, "somebody will cut it open."

"Stop it!" Cynthia screamed, clapping her hands over her ears.

She ran from the school yard and didn't stop until she was home. She pushed past Kevin, who was waiting for her on the porch. "No meeting today," she shouted, and then, in her bedroom, she burst into tears.

## The Natural-Born Knot Tie-er

It was a long time before Cynthia would come out of her room. When she did her eyes were red and swollen. She faced Albert, who had been knocking steadily and calling her name with growing concern.

"Rita's gone," she told him.

"Gone?" he echoed.

"Pet store," Cynthia mumbled. "From there it's the pound, then the lab — cut up in pieces."

Slowly she told him the whole story, and Albert sat down on his bed, his head in his hands. After several minutes of deep thought he looked up, smiling.

"If Rita's at a pet store, all we have to do is find out which one and buy her back."

"I don't have any money," Cynthia said dismally.

"We'll solve that problem next," Albert said briskly. "First things first. That's what you learn in Scouts."

In the yellow section of the telephone book they saw the long list of pet stores. But Albert said confidently, "We'll call them all."

After the tenth call Albert's voice grew husky. None of the storekeepers had a white rat named Rita. Some of them, in fact, were very cross at having to answer the telephone, thinking the call was just a prank. "I don't have a rat named Rita," grumbled one man, "and I don't have frogs' legs or rabbit feet either. I'm tired of you kids making jokes on the telephone!"

From then on Cynthia and Albert took turns telephoning.

"Pardon me," Cynthia said politely, when it was her turn. "Do you happen to have any rats?"

"Look, girlie," the man answered, "we got almost all kinds—chicken, lamb, beef, ham, but *rat*! Are you on some new kind of diet?"

Wordlessly Cynthia handed the receiver to Albert, who repeated the request. When he had finished Albert said, laughing, "You dialed wrong, you nut. That was Black's Butcher Shop."

By supper time they had called every store in the book. No Rita. After supper, when Daddy turned on the news, there was no Rita running on the treadmill. Later, when Mother came clomping down the stairs in her slippers, there was no Rita standing at the door of her cage.

Everything, in fact, reminded Cynthia of Rita. Even in the night she awakened, her thoughts turning immediately to Rita. Where are you, Rita? she wondered sadly. What's happened to you? Oh, Rita—you're not even a weekend rat now.

The next morning was bleak and gloomy, and Cynthia wandered around the house as if she were lost.

"Don't worry," Albert said gruffly, putting his arm around her shoulder. "We'll find Rita somehow. Look at it this way," he said encouragingly. "Since Rita isn't here this weekend, you don't have to clean her cage or anything. Without doing any work at all, you'll be one-third of the way through your bargain."

"Even if I find Rita," Cynthia reasoned, "this weekend won't count because she isn't here."

"*When* you find her," Albert said, "you can take care of her for Mrs. Hanson after school every day. That should make up for it."

"*If* I find her," Cynthia said. For the first time she had lost all hope.

"I guess I'll get busy on that garage," Albert said, looking back at Cynthia.

"I'll help you," she sighed. She had made a

promise to Daddy, and she would keep it. Miserable as she was already, the thought of cleaning the garage didn't seem to be so distasteful. Nothing seemed to matter.

Daddy had nailed the shelf back onto the wall. Albert had folded his pup tent neatly and placed it on the shelf. Everyone had helped to gather up the spilled nails.

Together Cynthia and Albert heaved up the boxes of Cynthia's rock collection and put them on another shelf. Odd shoes, boots, sand pails, and toy trucks were placed smartly in a row.

"It's not so bad," Albert mused, "except for these papers." They lay in scattered piles all over the garage. "Wish that Bruno would learn to put them in the same place each night," Albert grumbled. "It'll take us days to get this done."

For a moment Cynthia had a dim vision of the garage all clean and neat. Daddy would bring in the patio furniture, and her winter clubhouse would be all ready for use. But even that didn't seem to matter anymore. The wind groaned under the garage door and between the cracks around the window. Tree branches pushed restlessly against the outside wall. From far away a cat howled, a long, lonely sound.

Methodically they began stacking the papers. When the stack was tall enough they got the twine and began to wrap it around.

"This is the hard part," Albert said with a grunt. He bit his lip in concentration, attempting a knot, *any* knot. But as soon as he let go the twine slipped, as if with a nasty will of its own.

"We'll just start another stack," Albert said, turning away.

I'll never see Rita again, Cynthia was thinking to herself. Without realizing it, she had taken the ends of the twine, twisted them over, under, around, and there on top of the stacked papers was a perfect and secure square knot.

"Hey!" Albert cried in astonishment. "How'd you do that?"

"I don't know," Cynthia said quickly. "I guess I — I just did it."

"Let's see you do it again," Albert urged.

Quickly they prepared another stack of papers, and this time Cynthia tied it with a bowline.

Albert's eyes widened in amazement. "Hey! How'd you do that?"

"Well, it just sort of came to me," Cynthia stammered. "My fingers just — knew how."

"You," said Albert gravely, "are a genius. Not in everything, of course," he added quickly. "But you are a *natural-born knot tie-er*. People are born knowing all sorts of things," he continued seriously. "Some are born swimmers, some are born musicians, and you — you are a natural-born knot tie-er!" he said gleefully.

"I guess I am," Cynthia said, smiling slightly. "Maybe I could show you how. I make up stories about them in my mind."

"What stories?" Albert asked, his voice very intense.

Cynthia took up a piece of rope. "Here's one for the square knot," she said. She worked slowly, explaining, "This is the rabbit. Here are the ears. The rabbit sees a hunter coming. He turns around quick. He heads the other way. Now *pull*." Proudly she showed him the completed knot.

"Say," Albert murmured admiringly, "it doesn't seem hard at all when you put it that way. Let me try."

Slowly, carefully, repeating Cynthia's story word for word, Albert worked with the rope. "I did it!" he cried, leaping up into the air. "I did it! Quick. Fix another stack. I've got to do it again."

Soon three bundles were lined up side by side, each boasting a fine square knot. "Now show me the bowline," Albert begged. "I'll need to know that in case I have to rescue someone mountain climbing."

"This is the rabbit," Cynthia began, working with the rope tied around her waist, "this is the tree. This is the rabbit hole. The rabbit comes out of the hole. He goes around the tree, back in the hole, then *pull*."

"It's simple," Albert grinned, when he had made a bowline perfectly. "This rabbit thing really does the trick. I know I can learn the others, now that I've got the idea!"

Albert rushed upstairs, searching for more newspapers to tie. He gathered papers from under the kitchen sink, from shelves and tables. He even snatched up the weekend paper, although it was still Saturday, and nobody had read it yet.

"Leave that alone, Albert," Daddy said.

"I can tie!" Albert exclaimed. "I can tie!"

"You mean — real knots?" Daddy asked in amazement.

"Come and see."

Daddy surveyed the garage. He shook his head in wonder. Seven bundles of newspapers, all neatly tied, lined the wall. Two bundles of magazines stood under the work bench.

Daddy gazed at Cynthia, then at Albert. "Children," he said, "I am speechless." But he managed to make a rather long speech about people helping each other and people sticking to their jobs and people planning ahead. Mother, too, came to admire the clean garage, nodding happily.

Everyone's happy, Cynthia thought, except for me.

Albert rushed around the house testing his new skill. He tied the clothesline to a tree. He tied his chair to his desk. He tied his shoelaces together.

"Want me to tie something for you?" he asked Cynthia.

Cynthia shook her head.

71

"Let's go over to Mrs. Aimsley's house," he
suggested. "Maybe she wants some papers tied.
I've got to keep in practice, you know."

Cynthia didn't want to go to Mrs. Aimsley's
house. Mrs. Aimsley somehow reminded her of
Rita. "Where do you think she is?" she sighed.

"Right next door, of course, you nut."

"I mean Rita."

"Listen," Albert said gently, "if you don't find
Rita on Monday, maybe you can save up and buy
another rat. I've got fifty-eight cents I'll give you."

"I don't want another rat," Cynthia said, her
voice trembling. "I just want Rita."

"I know," Albert said softly. "But you can't just

sit around and mope. Let's go to Mrs. Aimsley's."

Mrs. Aimsley gathered up newspapers from her house and garage. Albert and Cynthia got the red wagon, brought Mrs. Aimsley's papers into their garage, and tied them up too.

"It's starting to look like a Cub Scout paper drive in here," Albert mumbled when they had finished.

At last the long weekend was over. As Cynthia walked to school on Monday morning she wondered how she would ever get through the school day. Mrs. Hanson did not begin teaching kindergarten until ten. And children from the other grades were not allowed in the kindergarten area during school hours.

Usually Cynthia played wall ball in the mornings before the bell rang. But she wasn't taking any chances today. She went straight to the classroom and sat at her desk, remembering what a long, lonely weekend it had been without Rita.

All Sunday she had stayed indoors, not knowing what to do with herself. She didn't want to see Kevin or Benny or Pete. She would have to explain what happened on Friday, and somehow she simply couldn't. What if the boys teased her and said, "You're a big sissy worrying about an old rat!" And when Mother suggested that she play with Betty Filbert, Cynthia shook her head sadly.

"I have no friends," she told Mother. "The boys

don't like me because I'm a girl, and the girls don't like me because I'm a tomboy."

"There's nothing wrong with being a girl," Mother had said gently. *"I'm* a girl."

"Girls are sissies!" Cynthia had retorted angrily.

"Girls are anything they want to be," Mother had said. "They can be brave and strong and still enjoy things like baking cookies." And Mother had let Cynthia help her bake. That had been the only good thing about the whole weekend.

Cynthia sighed deeply, wishing the school day would begin, so she could start counting recesses until it was over.

"What's wrong, Cynthia?" said a soft voice behind her.

Cynthia looked up, startled. She hadn't heard Betty Filbert come in.

"Nothing," Cynthia said listlessly. And then, "Everything—*everything* is wrong." And before she knew it, she had told Betty all about Rita and her bargain with Daddy and about seeing Joe Tomkins on Friday afternoon.

"That's terrible," Betty sympathized. "But maybe Joe Tomkins was lying. That Joe Tomkins is always doing mean things. He's the meanest boy in school."

"He sure is!" Cynthia agreed stoutly. Somehow she felt better having told Betty about it all.

"Maybe he really didn't know anything about

Rita," Betty went on. "Maybe he was just mad that you won the fight with Benny."

"I — I *won* the fight?" Cynthia marveled.

"Sure," Betty said admiringly. "You knocked Benny flat, didn't you? I bet you'll find Rita," Betty said reassuringly.

"If I do," Cynthia said, "do you want to see her some time?"

"Sure. I love little animals."

"So do I," Cynthia said.

"I like rocks, too," Betty went on. "I've got a big rock collection."

"So do I!" Cynthia exclaimed. "Hey, do you want to look for rocks during recess?"

"Oh, yes," Betty replied, smiling broadly. "And maybe some day we can trade. I've got lots of extras."

The day didn't seem so terribly long after all, with recesses to look forward to. During lunchtime Cynthia ate with Betty, and by the time the lunch recess was over Cynthia decided she really would have Betty over so they could trade rocks. Maybe, she thought to herself, she'd do it on a day when the boys were all away.

Finally the last bell rang and Cynthia rushed straight to Mrs. Hanson's room.

"Why, Cynthia!" Mrs. Hanson said with surprise. "I thought you were sick. Why didn't you come for Rita last Friday? I had an appointment after school and I couldn't wait any longer so . . . "

Cynthia looked over to the shelf. There was the cage. And inside the cage were not one, but *two* identical white rats.

"Rita!" Cynthia cried. "There are two of her!"

"It certainly looks that way," Mrs. Hanson laughed. "Actually, there is only one Rita. The other rat belongs to Stuart Brooks. He took Rita to his house last Friday when you didn't come for her."

"Joe Tomkins *did* lie," Cynthia muttered to herself.

"Since Stuart has a rat, too," Mrs. Hanson continued, "he decided to put them both in the same cage, to let them play together. Now we have a problem. We can't tell which rat is which."

Cynthia moved closer to the cage. She called Rita's name. Neither of the rats moved. They were huddled together, resting.

"It's that one," Cynthia said, pointing. "No, I guess it's the other one. I'm not sure."

She took each rat out and held it, petted it, but still she couldn't tell them apart. "I give up," Cynthia said at last, shaking her head. "Still, they *are* different. There *has* to be a difference," she insisted.

"Stuart is very upset," said Mrs. Hanson. "He wants his own rat back."

Cynthia nodded. She examined both rats again.

Rita had a small gray spot on her tail. She looked at both tails closely. Both had a small gray spot.

"Different rats would *act* different," she said slowly, thinking hard.

"How?" Mrs. Hanson asked. "Is there anything special Rita does?"

Suddenly Cynthia exclaimed. "Of course! I know how we can tell! Will you wait here for me, Mrs. Hanson? I have to run home and get something. I'll be right back."

# Who Brought the Plague to England?

When Cynthia got back to Mrs. Hanson's room, she took off her shoes and put on her mother's slippers. Mrs. Hanson watched with a puzzled look.

"They clomp," Cynthia explained, taking several steps. She walked toward the cage, letting the slippers clomp loudly. Suddenly one of the rats jumped up and darted over to the cage door, standing up eagerly.

"That's Rita!" Cynthia cried, reaching in to grasp her. She kissed Rita's head again and again, then laid the rat against her shoulder. Rita gave a sniffle, then a mighty sneeze. "It's Rita," Cynthia repeated happily. "I'm sure."

"Amazing," said Mrs. Hanson. "That rat has *learned*."

"She is very smart," Cynthia said modestly.

"And you are a good teacher," Mrs. Hanson smiled. "You really deserve to have Rita for your own."

"I have to take her home three more weekends," Cynthia sighed, "unless I can come in after school every day and clean the cage and feed her."

"I'm afraid that wouldn't work," the teacher said. "I can't stay after school long enough every day for that. But three weekends isn't so very long. If I know you, you'll keep busy and the time will go fast."

Mrs. Hanson gave Cynthia a small calendar. "Why don't you use this to mark off the days," she suggested. "You'll see how fast they go. Look!" she exclaimed, pointing to the calendar. "Three more weekends and it will be Halloween."

Cynthia's eyes shone. "Halloween weekend," she murmured. "Rita will be mine on Halloween weekend, the same weekend that Albert gets into Scouts."

"Sounds like two good reasons for a party," Mrs. Hanson remarked. She took Rita from Cynthia's arms. "I'll call Stuart and have him get his own rat. I'll hold onto Rita until he gets here. We wouldn't want that mix-up again!"

As she walked home, Cynthia repeated the

magic-sounding words to herself. *Halloween weekend . . . Halloween weekend.* Mrs. Hanson was right. It was a perfect time for a party. And a big party was just the right kind of project for the club.

That very afternoon Cynthia called a special meeting. As they discussed the plans, the party became bigger and better by the minute.

Games! They would have relay races, running races, and of course rat races, with prizes for the winners.

Costumes! Everyone would come in costume, with prizes for the best.

Booths! They would have a ring toss, ducking for apples, popping balloons. Of course, there would be prizes for the winners.

"Where are we going to get all that money for prizes?" Pete asked skeptically.

Everyone fell silent, brooding.

"Club dues," Kevin suggested.

"That's not enough," said Pete.

"We can use apples from my tree," Kevin offered.

"Fine," said Cynthia. "But what about the other things? Where do we get prizes and decorations and balloons?"

"I've got lots of balloons," Benny said loudly, "all colors. I saved them from my last birthday party. We can use those," he said, smiling and nodding with satisfaction.

"Great!" everyone shouted.

Then Benny took off his glasses. He slid his thumb over the lens. "I forgot," he muttered. "I was *going* to save them. I put them all in a box. I wasn't going to blow them up. I wasn't going to stick pins in them to hear them pop."

Now there was a dreamy look on his face. "I blew one up. There's something about a balloon getting bigger and bigger...feeling the air go in. And then, when you pop it with a pin..." He sighed. "I just couldn't stop. They're all gone. Popped."

Pete stamped his foot angrily. "Honestly, Benny, you're a..."

But Cynthia broke in. "Let's go play wall ball. We'll think of something. It's easier to think outside. The cold air wakes up your brains."

They ran out to play wall ball. But after a few minutes Mrs. Aimsley stuck her head out the window and shouted, "Stop that banging, children. I'm on-the-verge-of-a-nervous-breakdown! And Mr. Aimsley is coming home soon with his truck. Go away! Far away!"

As they turned to leave Mrs. Aimsley called again. "Cynthia! I have some more newspapers for you. Would you and your friends like to get them?"

Cynthia didn't really want to carry Mrs. Aimsley's newspapers back to her house, but she didn't want to be rude, either. "Yes, Mrs. Aimsley," she said, and when Mrs. Aimsley gave them the papers Cynthia told her a polite "Thank you."

81

"Why'd you thank her?" Pete grumbled. "This is just junk."

"Because she gave us something," Cynthia explained.

"What good are old newspapers?" Pete argued.

"Yeah," added Kevin. "She should thank us for taking them."

"Grown-ups sure think kids are dumb," added Benny. "Now we're stuck with a bunch of old papers."

"Albert will tie them up," said Cynthia.

"So what?" Pete asked. "Then we're stuck with a bunch of dirty old *tied-up* newspapers."

They took the papers to the garage and set them down beside the other bundles.

Benny gave a whistle. "Gee whiz, you've sure got lots of papers."

"Come on," said Pete impatiently. "Let's do something. I thought this club was gonna be fun. All we do is..."

"Order! Order!" Cynthia screamed, and everyone stared at her.

"What's wrong?" they asked, for Cynthia looked as if she were going to burst. The most wonderful idea had just popped into her head.

"We'll collect newspapers!" she exclaimed. "We'll sell them. We'll get *lots* of money. Then we can have our party and get prizes and booths and *everything*."

So great was the excitement, so loud were the shouts, that Bruno slammed himself against the side door until Cynthia let him into the garage. Then he ran round and round in circles, barking wildly. For five whole minutes the celebration continued. Then Pete gave a loud groan.

"Who wants to buy old newspapers, anyway?" he asked.

"Paper company," Cynthia replied.

"Why would they?" Pete argued.

"They just do!" Cynthia snapped.

"How will we get enough papers?"

"We'll go collecting."

"If people can get money for their old papers," Pete reasoned, "why would they give them to us? Why wouldn't they sell their own?"

"Because they don't have a wagon," Cynthia said firmly. "You've got to have wagons to go collecting. Do you all have wagons?"

"Yes!" they all roared, and Benny boasted of having a tremendous wagon with huge wheels. But, *but* . . .

"I forgot," said Benny. "I took it apart. I never put it back together again. One of the wheels got lost, so . . ."

"Never mind, Benny!" Cynthia shouted, glaring. Then she added more calmly, "You can share my wagon."

Before they left, Cynthia instructed the boys to

save all their newspapers. "Tell your friends. Tell your neighbors. And you can bring them to my garage anytime."

Slowly the paper drive began. The boys told their parents. They told their neighbors. Neighbors told other neighbors, and the word went along the streets. "Save your papers. There's a bunch of kids who'll pick 'em up for free."

A few papers more or less in that garage already filled with papers were not noticed at all. Neither Mother nor Daddy nor Albert knew anything about the paper drive. Cynthia decided to keep it a secret. They would know soon enough. Meanwhile she marked her calendar every day, and the first weekend of the bargain was half over. Everything was working out perfectly. Then came Miss Flagstaff.

"Tidy up your rooms," Mother said late on Saturday afternoon. "Miss Flagstaff is coming tonight."

Mother often spoke of Miss Flagstaff to her friends. "She's a most reliable baby sitter," Mother would say proudly. "She's neat as a pin, and she always puts the children to bed on time."

Albert and Cynthia groaned and exchanged glances. Mother often said, "Miss Flagstaff is a person of sound ideas."

"If she has any more 'sound ideas,' " moaned Albert, "I'll leave home."

"Just go wash your hands, young man," Mother said sternly.

"Last time Miss Flagstaff had a 'sound idea,' " Cynthia mumbled, "we didn't get any soda pop for a month."

"Miss Flagstaff told me that soda pop isn't good for children," Mother replied. "Now, you be nice, Cynthia."

Still they complained. "Miss Flagstaff treats us like babies," said Albert. "She just plays baby games, like blowing bubbles. Who ever heard of an old lady blowing bubbles all the time?"

"She cheats," Cynthia added heatedly. "The only card game she knows is 'Fish,' and she'll do anything to win."

"She uses up all our bubble bath," Albert went on.

Daddy came in grinning. "I'd better wash my ears before Miss Flagstaff comes," he said. "Last time she looked as if she was going to take me by the scruff of the neck and march me over to the sink."

"Charles!"Mother said warningly. "It wouldn't hurt any of us to try to learn a thing or two from Miss Flagstaff. Are you ready, Charles? Let's not be late for the party."

The doorbell rang. It was Miss Flagstaff, wearing the brown beanie-shaped hat she always wore.

"Here we are!" Miss Flagstaff said brightly,

nodding to Mother. But as she stepped inside the door she stopped abruptly. A strange look came over Miss Flagstaff's face. She sniffed. She sniffed again.

"What do you suppose," she asked with a puzzled look, "that odd smell could be?"

"It's not me!" Albert said. "I don't need a bath."

"Hush, Albert," Mother said sharply. Then, to Miss Flagstaff, "I don't smell anything."

"We're used to it," Cynthia said. "It's Rita. We don't smell her anymore."

"Rita?" Miss Flagstaff blinked rapidly.

"My rat," explained Cynthia. "That is, she's almost mine. I just have to..."

"Rat," Miss Flagstaff repeated woodenly.

"Would you like to see her?" Cynthia asked eagerly.

"*Rat*," Miss Flagstaff repeated, and now Cynthia saw that her face had gone pale.

"It's in a cage," Mother said quickly.

"It's a pet," Daddy added, "and quite tame."

Miss Flagstaff stood firmly in the doorway. She held onto her hat with both hands. It looked as if she had no intention of staying.

"Perhaps you are not aware of the fact," Miss Flagstaff said slowly, "that rats are carriers of *disease*. They have been responsible for the death of *thousands* of human beings."

Nobody said anything. They all stared at Miss

Flagstaff, and Cynthia saw that Mother was frowning, wringing her hands nervously.

"Who brought the plague to England?" Miss Flagstaff demanded.

"Not Rita," Cynthia said in a small voice.

"*Rats*," declared Miss Flagstaff. "That's how the plague came to England. Which animal is man's worst enemy? Rats," Miss Flagstaff concluded.

"You don't have to go near the rat, Miss Flagstaff," Mother said. "I'm sorry it upsets you."

"I should say it does upset me." Miss Flagstaff shivered. "To think that people would make pets of *those things*. To think that a child would handle one of *those things*."

Cynthia clenched her fists behind her back and gritted her teeth. *How dare she?* Cynthia thought, feeling furious. But Mother had put on her coat and was speaking soothingly to the baby sitter.

"We must go now, Miss Flagstaff. We have some new bubble bath," Mother coaxed.

"I simply cannot understand how people can..." Miss Flagstaff sputtered.

"It's very nice," Mother murmured. "Green pine."

Miss Flagstaff sniffed again. She took off her brown beanie hat and placed it carefully on the table. "Well," she said, "I did bring my bubble pipe. The children do so love to blow bubbles."

Albert and Cynthia only looked at each other.

Then, from down in the rumpus room, came a sniff, snuffle, sneeze.

"The rat sneezes," Daddy said. "Don't try to watch the news. It's useless."

Miss Flagstaff drew herself up very straight. "That rat," she declared, "is obviously sick. The children must not touch it. If I were you," she told Mother, "I would make a full report to the Public Health Department. I can only hope you will decide to..."

Cynthia heard no more, for she ran upstairs to her room. A few minutes later she heard Mother and Daddy leave. Then Miss Flagstaff knocked loudly at Cynthia's door.

"I will not blow bubbles," Cynthia called out. "I will not play 'Fish.' "

"Suit yourself," replied Miss Flagstaff through the door. "Come on, Albert. Your deal. Do you remember how to play?"

## Mountains of Papers

Rita's cage did not get cleaned on Sunday.

"I'm not taking any chances with our health," Mother said. "Miss Flagstaff could be right."

"Now, Molly," said Daddy, "nobody gets plague anymore. Miss Flagstaff is just too fussy."

"She was right that time Cynthia had the measles," Mother retorted, looking very distressed. "The children are *not* to go near Rita until I've checked with the vet."

"Then how can I feed her?" Cynthia asked tearfully.

"I'll feed her myself," Mother said, "without touching her."

"But it's part of my bargain," Cynthia said.

90

"Don't worry about that," Daddy said. "We just won't count today." He took Cynthia aside and whispered, "It'll be all right. Your mother is just worried. I'm sure Rita is fine."

"Miss Flagstaff wants us to get rid of Rita," Cynthia cried. "She'd kill Rita if she could. The only reason she didn't kill her last night was because she was afraid to get close to her."

"You could be right," Daddy said grimly. He went into the kitchen and closed the door. Cynthia could hear the rumble of their voices, but she couldn't make out the words. Many minutes later Mother came out.

"Daddy and I have discussed this," she told Albert and Cynthia. "We have decided to try a new baby sitter for a change."

Albert and Cynthia cheered and grinned.

"But," Mother continued, "what I said about Rita still goes. I won't take any chances. We'll call Dr. Caldwell first thing in the morning."

Right after breakfast Mother telephoned Dr. Caldwell, the veterinarian. Daddy, Albert, and Cynthia stood around her, listening.

Cynthia felt as if she were hearing a conversation backwards. As Mother answered, she knew what Dr. Caldwell's questions had been.

"How old is the rat?" was the first question.

"About a year," Mother said.

"What are the symptoms?" the vet asked.

"She sneezes a lot."

"What do you feed her?" came next.

"Rat food. Crusts of bread." Mother turned and asked Cynthia. "Anything else?"

"Carrots," Cynthia replied, "and cheese. Yellow cheese, especially when she wins the race."

"Carrots," Mother said into the telephone receiver. "And cheese."

Mother listened intently, nodding her head, frowning. Then she said, "I see, Doctor. Very well. I will. We won't. Thank you. Good-bye."

Mother sat down in a chair, while everyone stood around her.

"What is it?" they all asked.

"Cheese," Mother said. Then her lips spread into a grin, until she laughed out loud. "Cheese!" she declared. "That's what's causing the sneezing. Rats shouldn't eat cheese," she exclaimed. "They're allergic to it."

"But — but," Cynthia stammered, "I thought rats love cheese."

"Maybe they do," Mother said, still chuckling, "but it's not good for them. Dr. Caldwell was very firm about that. He told me, 'It's all because of that silly song about the rat taking the cheese. It's made people think that rats should have cheese. Well, they're wrong. Dead wrong.' "

"Then there's nothing really wrong with Rita at all!" Cynthia said.

"Nothing," Mother echoed. "Just stop feeding her cheese." She turned to Daddy, smiling wistfully, "Oh, Charles, I feel so foolish."

"Not at all," Daddy said, beaming. "That means I can hear the news again. Now, off to work. Off to school. I'll drive you to school," he told Cynthia and Albert, "and Rita too, of course."

It had begun with a trickle, and the trickle grew into a torrent. Two newspapers came from Kevin's little sister Sara. Benny came carrying an armful of newspapers; Pete had a wagon full. Then people began calling on the telephone. Strange voices asked, "Are you the little girl who is collecting newspapers?"

"Yes," Cynthia would reply eagerly. "Give me your address. We'll come and get them as soon as we can."

On Tuesday all club members went out with their wagons to collect newspapers.

On Wednesday there were so many calls that Cynthia had to stay home to answer the telephone. In a steady stream she sent the boys from one address to another. And the calls kept coming.

By Thursday it was no longer a secret. Mother was on-the-verge... "Cynthia!" she exclaimed, "that telephone is driving me crazy. And what will your father say when he sees that garage?"

That night Daddy came in with a roar. The sight

of that garage, he groaned, left him speechless. Then he spoke for a long, long time. At the end of his speech he sent Albert and Cynthia upstairs.

"You sure got me into a mess," Albert burst out at Cynthia. "Now we've got to clear out all those papers before the investiture. It's just a week and two days away. Don't you ever finish anything?" He paced back and forth angrily. "Don't you ever plan ahead?"

"I *have* planned ahead," Cynthia shouted back. "All you have to do is help me tie up those papers. I helped you," she reminded him. "I showed you how to tie those knots."

Albert slumped down on his bed. "Do you realize," he asked, "how many papers you'll need before you can make any money selling them? Tons and *tons*. I asked my Scout leader. You only get nine dollars a ton. And a ton is *two thousand pounds!*"

"I know that," Cynthia shouted. "I know all about it." But really, she hadn't known at all. She tried to imagine how many newspapers it would take to make a ton. She pictured mountains and mountains of newspapers. It seemed impossible. She only weighed fifty-five pounds. How could a fifty-five pound person collect two thousand pounds of anything?

"And how will you get those papers hauled away?" Albert demanded.

"I've got that all planned," Cynthia snapped. This wasn't exactly true; in fact, she had no plan at all. "First things first," she told Albert. "That's what you learned in Scouts. Just help me tie up those papers and leave everything else to me."

All evening Cynthia brooded. How many pounds does one stack weigh? How many stacks make a ton? If the papers keep coming, how can we tie them fast enough? And when they're all tied, who will take them to the paper company? All the next day during school Cynthia still brooded. She doodled on her paper. She daydreamed during the spelling lesson. She frowned and bit her pencils and drummed her fingers on her desk.

"What's wrong, Cynthia?" Betty Filbert asked. "Are you sick? You keep groaning to yourself."

"I just can't do it," Cynthia whispered back. "There's not enough time. I don't have enough helpers...."

Miss Klampert gave Cynthia a sharp glance, and Cynthia turned back to her work with a deep sigh. When the bell rang for lunch recess, Cynthia walked out with Betty. While they ate, she told Betty everything.

"You need a truck," Betty mused, frowning. "If my dad had a truck I'd ask him to help you."

"Thanks anyway," Cynthia mumbled. Betty was trying to help, but what Cynthia really needed was several extra pairs of hands.

"Can you tie knots?" she asked Betty.

"Not very well," Betty admitted. "But I could answer the telephone for you. Then you'd have more time to tie papers."

So after school Betty came with Cynthia to pick up Rita. "What a sweet little thing!" Betty exclaimed. She stayed long enough to hold Rita, to cuddle her against her cheek, and then she ran home to change.

When Betty came back Cynthia was astonished to see that she, too, was wearing boys' jeans.

"Where'd you get the boys jeans?" she asked.

"My mother bought them for me last week," Betty replied, looking embarrassed.

"How come?" Cynthia asked. "I never saw you wearing jeans before. Are you a tomboy now?"

"I — I don't know," Betty said hesitantly. "Do you want me to be?"

Cynthia did not know what to say. Nor was

there time to answer, for at that moment Pete, Benny, and Kevin came up the street with their wagons clattering. Kevin's wagon was so full that Sara, his little sister, had to sit on top to keep the papers from sliding off.

When the boys had unloaded their wagons, they all stood around surveying the garage. Single pages of newspaper spilled out into the driveway, where they flapped and fluttered with every ripple of the autumn wind. Piles of newspapers lay on top of old chairs, in cartons, on shelves. Mounds of newspapers cluttered the corners. Mountains of papers blocked the doorways, and still they kept on coming.

A woman Cynthia had never seen before pulled up in the driveway, her station wagon loaded with bundled newspapers.

"This must be the place," the children heard her say. With her was her son, and the moment they came into earshot Cynthia heard the mother scolding, "Why don't you ever do anything helpful? Look what these children are doing. They've got ambition. Now hurry and unload those papers!"

The boy said nothing. He fell to work, unloading twelve bundles of newspapers, all neatly tied. All the while his mother kept scolding.

"Do you want to stay here for a while and help us?" Cynthia asked, smiling.

The boy returned a smile of relief. "Sure do," he said. "My mom's been after me ever since she heard about this paper drive of yours."

The boy's name was Conrad. He fell to work at once, stacking and tying papers. Then Albert came home and pitched in. Soon a production line was organized.

Betty received the telephone calls and Sara came running down to the garage with the messages. Then Cynthia would dispatch Pete, Kevin, or Benny to pick up more papers.

That night when Daddy came home he really was speechless. Fifty-nine bundles of newspapers filled one whole side of the garage.

"Don't say anything, Charles," Mother said quickly, meeting him at the door. "You'll just have to keep your car outside for a few days."

"How..." Daddy began, but Mother drew him aside. Her voice was low, but Cynthia heard the words.

"Let the children finish this their own way, Charles. I know it looks impossible, but I think they'll manage — somehow."

"I have only one thing to say," Daddy declared. "This whole thing had better be over by next Friday afternoon."

On Sunday night Cynthia made another X on the calendar Mrs. Hanson had given her. Only one more weekend remained, and then Rita would be hers.

She lay down on her bed, feeling aches in every muscle. Her arms and back were weary from carrying newspapers. Her fingers were sore from tying the twine. Her hands, knees, and face had been so stained with newsprint that it took many scrubbings to get them clean. But although she was more tired than she could ever remember, and although she still did not know how to get rid of the papers, she was happy.

All through the weekend the boys had worked. Even Conrad had come back to help.

But of all the children, Betty Filbert had worked the hardest. She had stayed on Sunday afternoon long after the boys went home, helping to tidy up the garage. Then Cynthia had showed Betty how Rita could race, how she reacted to the clomp of slippers on the stairs, and Betty had sighed wistfully.

"You're so lucky Cynthia," Betty had said. "I

wish I had a rat. I don't have any pets." Betty held Rita while Cynthia cleaned the cage.

"She sure is a fat little rat," Betty murmured.

"She eats a lot," Cynthia replied. She too had noticed that Rita seemed to be a little heavier. "Maybe," she said, "I ought to put her on a diet."

And then Rita had done something new. Cynthia had left a small scrap of paper in the bottom of the cage. Immediately Rita snatched the paper and proceeded to tear it into little bits. One by one she took the tiny scraps and laid them in a small pile in the corner. Then she ran to the cage door, standing up eagerly.

"She wants more paper," Betty said in amazement.

Cynthia gave Rita a piece of the funnies. Soon that too was torn into little bits and piled up on top of the others. Then Rita turned around two or three times and curled up right on top of the soft newspaper nest.

"Maybe she's getting ready for winter," Betty said.

"Maybe," Cynthia echoed, but she began to wonder. What makes an animal start building a nest?

## If You Want to Be a Girl Scout

Word went around the neighborhood.

"Kevin's club is collecting papers."

"Pete wants old newspapers."

"Call Cynthia. She'll get your papers."

Thus the newspapers kept coming. Cynthia and Albert spent each afternoon bundling them. Daddy kept shaking his head, saying nothing, keeping his car outside at night.

On Wednesday Mother took Albert downtown to buy his Boy Scout uniform. The night before he had shown Daddy that he could tie every knot listed in the Scout book.

As Cynthia sat down on Albert's bed, watching him adjust his cap and neckerchief again and again she wished with all her heart that she were a boy. The uniform was splendid from the crisp cap right down to Albert's highly polished shoes.

"How do I look?" asked Albert, beaming with pride.

"Perfect," said Cynthia, sighing. She could just picture Albert at the investiture, sitting together with the other Scouts, saying the Scout oath, making plans for hikes and cook-outs and wonderful projects.

"I guess you'll have lots of friends now," Cynthia said wistfully.

"*All* Scouts are buddies," Albert nodded, puffing out his chest.

"Betty Filbert says I could join her Scout troop," Cynthia said.

"Why don't you?" Albert asked, examining his new Scout knife.

"Do you want me to join Girl Scouts?"

"Why would I care?"

"Would you be glad if I were a Girl Scout?" Cynthia persisted.

"Look, Cynthia, people join clubs because they want to," Albert said seriously. "It's entirely up to you. Either you want to be part of it, or you don't. Do you want to go on hikes and cook-outs? Do you want to be on the softball team?"

"Girl Scouts don't do those things," Cynthia said. "*I* haven't seen them. All they do is sit around at meetings."

"That's because the troop is just getting organized," Albert explained. "How would you know what they really do? You're always off somewhere digging holes with those boys. I know even the Brownies have a softball team in the spring. I've seen them playing. And on our last Cub Scout hike we saw a Girl Scout troop..."

Suddenly Cynthia began to cry.

"What's wrong with you?" Albert muttered.

Still Cynthia sobbed, and Mother called, "Albert, what's wrong with Cynthia? Did you hit her?"

"I didn't touch her!" Albert yelled back. "Good grief," he said, "you're the nuttiest girl I ever saw. What are you crying about?"

"I want to be a Scout," Cynthia wept, "but the boys will tease me. If I wear that Girl Scout dress to school they'll laugh at me. They'll say, 'Oh, look at the little sissy!' "

"So what if they laugh?" Albert retorted. "Can't you take it? I thought you were brave."

"I *am* brave," Cynthia burst out. "I beat up Benny; I knocked him flat."

"That's not being brave," Albert said scornfully. "Being brave is..." Albert paused, then he picked up a small book lying on his desk. He waved it at Cynthia, and she saw the title, "Famous Heroes."

"This whole book is about people who did what they wanted to, even when other people laughed at them." Albert flipped the pages. "Thomas Edison!" he exclaimed. "A hero ... Johnny Appleseed ... George Washington Carver ... "

"*Heroes,*" Cynthia whispered in amazement.

"So go ahead and be a Girl Scout," Albert said with a grand sweep of his arm. "You can be anything you want. I'd kind of like to see you wearing a Scout uniform," he added, "instead of borrowing my shirts all the time."

All that evening Cynthia thought about it. And the more she thought about it, the more she wanted to be a Girl Scout. But a person didn't change from being a tomboy to being a *girl* all at once. It was the kind of thing you had to do slowly, gradually. First you gave up the boys' black socks. Then you wore a girl's shirt with your blue jeans. Then one day, no jeans at all, but pink shorts. After that, Cynthia pondered to herself, who knows? Maybe I'll even wear a bow in my hair—a very tiny one.

Cynthia decided to begin slowly, the very next day. After school she put on a white blouse with her jeans, though she still combed her hair down flat and wore Albert's baseball cap. When the boys arrived, pulling their wagons behind them, they didn't even notice that Cynthia was wearing a blouse instead of Albert's baseball shirt.

"That's all," Cynthia said. "No more newspapers. Let's just tie up what we have, and then we'll count."

"I'm tired of this," Benny frowned, sitting down on a pile of papers.

"Work, work, work," groaned Kevin.

"The guys asked me to go play football this afternoon," Pete put in. "I've got a new football helmet."

From down the street they heard voices, and they all looked up. It was Betty Filbert, and with her were two other girls. She had brought her sister, Megan, and Megan's friend, Pat, to help.

"Since we have to have everything done by tomorrow," Betty explained, "I thought you could use some extra people." She smiled toward the boys and said, "Hi! Let's get started."

Benny did not move from the spot.

"*Girls!*" Kevin groaned.

"I'm gettin' out of here," announced Pete.

The next minute they were gone, and the girls looked at each other, speechless. Megan knew how to tie knots, so they fell to work, two stacking, two tying knots. With Albert's help they were finished just before suppertime, and Cynthia stood back surveying the collection.

Before her was a solid wall of newspapers, stacked like great building blocks. The wall was taller than Albert, wider than all the children standing side by side.

"Did we do all that?" Cynthia marveled.

"It's impossible," Albert grinned, "but you did

it. But if you'd had to depend on your Boys' Club to finish up, you'd be in a pretty big mess right now."

"I'm sure glad you came," Cynthia told the girls gratefully.

"Oh, it was fun," Betty said.

"What was all this for?" Megan wanted to know.

Now Cynthia explained about the club and the Halloween party they were planning to have. Before she realized what she was saying, Cynthia blurted out, "You're all invited to come to the party on Saturday afternoon." It was only fair, she thought. They had helped with the work, so they should enjoy the party. But how would she ever get the boys to stand for it?

"We'd love to come," Betty said, speaking for all of them. "And you can come to the next Girl Scout meeting if you want to. Just to visit," she added, "and maybe you'll decide to join."

"Maybe," Cynthia said. And then, "Yes. I'd like to join."

Albert broke in. "Now, genius," he said to Cynthia, "how are you going to get all these papers out of here?"

"I haven't really thought about that," Cynthia admitted.

"You'll think of something," Betty said assuringly. "We have to go," she added to the girls. And when they were gone Cynthia picked up her ball and started bouncing it thoughtfully.

She walked outside with it. A little game of wall ball, she thought to herself, is what I need to help me think. Still bouncing the ball she walked over to Mrs. Aimsley's house. Maybe Mrs. Aimsley wouldn't mind. Maybe she was out. It seemed downright unfair that the very best driveway for playing wall ball was owned by people who didn't have any children.

She let the ball bounce. She smacked it back against the Aimsleys' garage door. Bounce. Bam. Bounce. Bang.

"Cynthia!" Mrs. Aimsley poked her head out the window.

At that very moment Cynthia heard the sharp blast of a horn behind her.

"Cynthia! Go play someplace else! Here comes Mr. Aimsley with his truck."

Cynthia stood aside as Mr. Aimsley pulled his truck into his driveway. She watched him get out. Then she knew what she must do.

"Mr. Aimsley!" she shouted. "Mr. Aimsley!"

"Yes, Cynthia," he said in his soft, patient voice.

"Mr. Aimsley," she said, breathing hard, "I would like to borrow your truck."

Mr. Aimsley's heavy eyebrows shot up. "*Would* you?" He studied Cynthia from the visor of her baseball cap down to the tips of her sneakers. "Do you know how to drive a truck?" he inquired.

"Well, no," Cynthia said, holding back a giggle.

"Then you want to borrow a truck *and* a driver, is that it?"

"Well, yes, Mr. Aimsley."

"That's better," he said. "Make yourself clear. Now tell me, why do you need a truck and a driver?" driver?"

"I have some newspapers to take to the paper company," Cynthia replied.

"How many?" Mr. Aimsley asked.

"Would you like to see?" Cynthia offered.

"I would, indeed," Mr. Aimsley said gravely. "I've been wondering about all the activity around here this past week."

When he saw the newspapers, Mr. Aimsley gave out a long, low whistle.

"The paper company will pay us nine dollars a ton," Cynthia explained quickly. "Do you think we have a ton?"

"I think so," Mr. Aimsley nodded.

"So when they pay us," Cynthia went on eagerly, "we could pay you for delivering the paper for us."

"I see," Mr. Aimsley mused. "And how much did you want to pay?"

"Fifty cents an hour?" Cynthia asked. "That's what my mother pays me for pulling weeds. Anything more, she always says, is highway robbery."

Mr. Aimsley puckered his lips, appearing to be deep in thought. "That seems a fair price," he said. "However," he added, "I would like to get a fringe benefit."

"A — a fringe benefit?" Cynthia echoed.

"Oh, you know," nodded Mr. Aimsley, "something extra. Something personal."

Cynthia stared at Mr. Aimsley, wondering what in the world she owned that Mr. Aimsley would like to have. She hoped it wasn't the baseball cap, since that really belonged to Albert.

"All right," Cynthia said slowly. "What do you want?"

"A promise," replied Mr. Aimsley. "I want your promise, *in writing*, that you and your brother and your friends will never, *never* play wall ball against my garage door again. It upsets Mrs. Aimsley.

And it would certainly disturb our new baby."

"New baby?" Cynthia gasped. "Is Mrs. Aimsley getting a baby?"

"She is," Mr. Aimsley said proudly, "very soon."

Cynthia's eyes grew wider and wider. "Golly," she said, "that's wonderful." She smiled broadly. "It's almost like having a rat."

Mr. Aimsley looked puzzled. "Is it agreed then? About the papers, I mean?"

"Oh, yes," Cynthia nodded. "Just a minute, please."

Cynthia ran up to her room. When she returned, she handed Mr. Aimsley a large piece of paper on which she had printed the words, I WILL NOT PLAY WAL BALL ENY MORE ON YOR GARISH. NO OTHER PEEPLE WILL PLAY THAR ETHER. CYNTHIA.

"It's a deal," said Mr. Aimsley, pocketing the paper. "Ho! There's your dad," he said, and the two men shook hands. "I've just made a deal with your daughter, Charles," said Mr. Aimsley. "I'm going to deliver these papers for her tomorrow morning on my way to work."

"Guess I'll help you load them up, then," said Daddy with a wink. "I hope Cynthia made a fair bargain," he added.

"Very fair," said Mr. Aimsley. "I'm satisfied."


"Rita won't be back," Cynthia told Mrs. Hanson

that Friday afternoon. "This is the last weekend of my bargain. Starting Sunday night, Rita is mine for keeps."

"I'm very glad," said Mrs. Hanson. "I know you'll give her a good home."

"Too good, maybe," said Cynthia. "Rita is getting fat."

"I've been meaning to talk to you about that, Cynthia," said Mrs. Hanson. "I've been thinking— I mean, I've been wondering whether Rita might be . . . "

They were interrupted by the eager voices of Pete, Benny, and Kevin. "We've come to help you take Rita home," Pete called out.

"I'll carry the cage," Kevin offered.

"I'll take the sawdust," said Benny.

And Pete, rubbing his hand over his red hair, said gruffly, "We shouldn't have run out on you yesterday, Cynthia."

"That's all right," Cynthia said, although she had been very angry when it happened. "We got everything done and by tonight we'll have the money. So we'd better get home and start planning the party." She would tell the boys later about having invited Betty, Megan, and Pat. There were, in fact, several things she would tell the boys later. Later, tommorow, she would summon her courage and tell them—but for now they could all enjoy planning their party.

When they got to her house, Cynthia was surprised to see Mr. Aimsley's truck parked in her driveway.

"I figured the sooner I brought you your money," Mr. Aimsley said, his eyes twinkling, "the sooner I'd get paid. I took them to the Palmer Paper Company, as you said," he went on. "The price of paper, you know, goes up and down."

"Just like the stock market," Mother put in, smiling.

"This month," continued Mr. Aimsley, "the price is up to eleven dollars a ton."

"Eleven bucks!" Kevin exclaimed.

"You children," declared Mr. Aimsley, "collected a little over two tons of newspapers."

There was absolute silence. Then there was chaos, absolute ear-splitting chaos.

"So here's your money," Mr. Aimsley said, when the noise had died down. "Twenty-four dollars and fifty cents. Who's the treasurer of this club?" he asked.

Pete stepped forward.

"Here you are," said Mr. Aimsley, handing him the money.

"And here is your pay, Mr. Aimsley," said Cynthia, taking fifty cents from Pete and giving it to Mr. Aimsley.

"And don't forget about that promise," he said, waving to them all.

*"Twenty-four dollars!"* they said over and over again.

"We've got *too* much money!" Kevin said, dazed.

"What'll we *do* with it all?" Benny asked.

"Let's decide what we'll need for the party," Pete suggested. "Whatever is left over—well, we can save it for the next club project."

Cynthia was about to speak, but she decided to remain silent. She would tell them tomorrow, after the party. A person had to choose. A person couldn't be everything all at once. Tomorrow she would tell the boys that she could no longer be a member of the Boys' Club.

## Halloween Weekend

The very first thing Cynthia did on Saturday morning, even before breakfast, was to clean Rita's cage. When Cynthia slid out the tray under the cage, Rita scurried over to the little heap of shredded papers in the corner. She sat on top of them, fixing her shiny red eyes on Cynthia as if to say, "I made this nest for myself. You leave it alone!"

When Cynthia reached in to fill Rita's feeding dish, Rita struck out with her little paw, then retreated. Once again Cynthia reached out, dropped a handful of pellets into the dish, and then she felt a slight nip on her finger.

"Don't bite me!" she scolded. "What's wrong with you, Rita?"

Rita curled her long tail tightly around her body and stared at Cynthia.

"I won't take your nest away," Cynthia soothed. "I won't bother you at all. In fact, I'm very busy today." She really had to plan ahead, with the investiture at one o'clock and the party at three.

The rest of the morning was spent in a flurry of preparations. Into the garage went the patio furniture, barbecue table, benches, chairs. Out came the Halloween decorations from last year: a skeleton that glowed in the dark, the huge cardboard witch on a real broomstick, paper pumpkins, ghosts, and humpbacked black cats.

"Many hands make light work," Mother said gaily, as she popped large pans of cookies into the oven. Pete mixed huge pitchers of Kool-Aid. Kevin and Benny carved out real pumpkins. Albert and Cynthia blew up balloons for the balloon-popping game, while Daddy prepared a ring toss booth and washed out the old pickle crock to be used for apple bobbing.

"How many children are coming?" Mother asked again and again. Then one of the children would remember still another friend who had been invited, and Mother would begin counting all over again.

Betty and Megan came running in, shouting, "We brought a record of spooky sounds." They also brought a record player. "We can play it during the party," Betty said.

Pete turned, aghast, and sputtered, "Who told you—who said anything about...."

Cynthia stepped up boldly until she was inches away from Pete. "I invited them to the party," she said firmly. "Betty and Megan are coming. If it wasn't for them, there wouldn't be any party."

Pete opened his mouth, then snapped it shut.

"I'm not gonna dance with them!" Kevin said threateningly.

"Who said anything about dancing?" Cynthia demanded. "Maybe you want to dance, Kevin, but we don't."

"*I* don't want to dance," Kevin grumbled, blushing a deep red. Then he added, "If those girls are coming, I'm bringing Sara. She helped too."

"The more the merrier!" Mother chirped. "Let's hurry now," she said. "We'll have to leave for the Scout investiture soon. Albert, you'd better get ready. We'll finish the party tables."

Out came the party plates and cups that the children had bought with their club money. They set out the black and orange candy cups, paper hats, snappers, and favors. Then they brought down the box of prizes. On the tables they put the jack-o'-lanterns that Kevin and Benny had carved, and Daddy helped Cynthia hang a huge black rubber spider on a thread from the garage ceiling.

They all stepped back, admiring their work.

"To tell the truth," Daddy began, "I never

thought you could do it. All the patio furniture is in. All the newspapers are gone. And you children have raised a large amount of money. Albert has learned everything he needs to know for the investiture, and Cynthia has just about completed the bargain that will change Rita from a weekend guest to a permanent member of the family. I think you children deserve a lot of credit," he said with a broad smile.

"Cynthia plans to use the garage as a winter clubhouse," Mother said. "I think she's proved that she can take care of things very well." Then Mother asked, "What's the next club project, Cynthia?"

Cynthia felt her face become hot. She felt shaky inside. She wished her mother hadn't said anything. But now the boys were asking all at once, "Yeah, what's next, Cynthia? Have you got another club project? Gee, this will be a neat winter clubhouse."

Cynthia looked down at her shoes. Everyone was waiting for her answer. She didn't know how to explain, how not to hurt anybody's feelings or to keep them from laughing at her.

"I've been thinking about it," Cynthia began softly. "We've done lots of things. But it's hard to plan ahead all the time. I mean, I have to do everything or else you guys always say you'll quit the club."

"We just say that," Benny mumbled. "We don't mean it."

"Well, I want to go hiking," Cynthia said heatedly, "and I want to cook out. I want to have a uniform and real meetings where everybody comes and pays dues and helps. And if I wear that uniform to school, let people laugh at me! It won't bother me a bit!"

"What are you talking about?" Pete demanded. "Why are you so mad?"

"I'm not mad," Cynthia replied angrily, "but if I want to be a Scout, I will. And I'm *going* to join the Girl Scouts. So you'll all say I'm a sissy, and you don't want any sissy girls in your club. So," she said, taking a deep breath, "I quit the Boys' Club."

"You can't do that!" they all shouted at once, and suddenly Bruno began to bark from inside the rumpus room, and over the barking Albert yelled, "Hey! Come in here!"

"Hold it!" Daddy shouted, and there was a general settling down. "What's wrong, Albert?" he called.

But there was no answer from Albert. Daddy opened the door to the rumpus room. "What's wrong?" he asked again.

Everyone crowded through the door. Everyone gazed at Albert who stood bent over Rita's cage, staring and pointing.

"What is it?" Cynthia asked, alarmed.

"Listen," Albert whispered.

And then Cynthia heard it — faint rustling, stirring sounds, tiny distant squeaks, and as she drew close to the cage, Cynthia's eyes widened, her mouth fell open in amazement.

The wonder of it — the complete surprise. *"Babies!"* The word passed in awed whispers from one to the other.

"Rita's a mother," Cynthia said breathlessly.

"She certainly is," Mother said with a tender smile.

"Don't touch them," Daddy said. "She's worried about her babies. Look at her trying to clean them all at once." His voice was very low, and his hand on Cynthia's shoulder was very gentle.

"Let me see," Kevin begged.

"They're so *tiny*!" Betty exclaimed.

"Smaller than my little finger," murmured Megan.

"Rita, oh Rita," Cynthia crooned, "no wonder you wanted your nest. Oh, they're beautiful babies, and they all look exactly like you."

How many? Everyone wanted to know, and they strained to see. Four little pink tails wriggled at the end of four pinkish-white bodies scarcely bigger than a thimble. All four cuddled close to their mother, seeking her warmth. Rita turned, and under her paws a fifth head peeked out. From under a curl of newspaper came another little

wriggle as the sixth baby made its way toward
Rita.

"Six," Daddy said, looking down into the cage,
and then, "No, wait. There's another one right in
the feeding dish!" And even as he spoke, Rita
scurried over, took the seventh of her babies into
her mouth and carried it back to the newspaper
nest.

Now Bruno pushed his way between Cynthia and Daddy, raising his big black nose to sniff curiously as he walked around and around the cage. He kept a respectful distance, and at last he sat down on the floor with ears up and eyes alert.

"We'd better get going," Daddy said, looking at his watch. "Bruno will guard the new family."

But the boys could not take their eyes from Rita and her babies. "Oh, man," Kevin sighed, "cool."

"Lucky," Benny added wistfully.

"Seven baby rats!" Pete said over and over again.

"We'll see you after the investiture, boys," Mother said, walking toward the door. "The party starts at three. Cynthia, go put on a dress."

But Cynthia and the boys were deep in conversation.

"You didn't mean that about quitting the club, did you?" Pete asked, frowning.

"It wouldn't be any fun without you," Benny said.

"We need you," Kevin added.

"But I'm going to join the Girl Scouts," Cynthia began, looking from one to the other.

"But even if you're a Girl Scout," Pete pointed out, "we can still have our club."

"You don't have to be a tomboy *all* the time," Benny said seriously. "*Some* girls are all right."

Cynthia glanced over at Betty. A slight smile

began around the corners of her mouth, spreading to a grin that made her face glow.

"I guess I'll stay in the club then," Cynthia said. "Our next project," she announced, "will be to find good homes for Rita's babies after they are grown. I think all club members should get a baby rat. All in favor?"

"EYE!" exclaimed the boys.

"And I think one of them should go to Betty. All in favor?"

"EYE!" they shouted again.

"And we can use the money left from our paper drive to buy cages," Pete suggested.

"Eye!"

"That means we'll have three baby rats left over. What will we do with them?" Benny asked.

Now Daddy came forward. "I wouldn't worry about that, Benny," he said with a smile. "I have an idea that Cynthia will think of something."

"You're right," Cynthia said, giving her father a quick hug. She would think of something, but for now she was simply too happy to concentrate on anything.

"In view of the fact that Rita has a family," Daddy said, "I'd like to announce that she is now here for keeps. I wouldn't want Rita to worry about it," he added with a grin.

After the boys had left, and all during the Scout investiture, the magical words sang through Cynthia's thoughts. Halloween weekend—and Rita's mine for keeps. Halloween weekend—and Rita's a mother, too. Halloween weekend — and Albert looked so fine, reciting the oath with the other Boy Scouts. Halloween weekend—it would be, it *was*, without a doubt, the jolliest, biggest, grandest Halloween party that anyone ever had.

# APPLE® PAPERBACKS

## More books you'll love, filled with mystery, adventure, friendship, and fun!

### NEW APPLE TITLES

| | | | |
|---|---|---|---|
| ☐ 40284-6 | **Christina's Ghost** | Betty Ren Wright | $2.50 |
| ☐ 41839-4 | **A Ghost in the Window** | Betty Ren Wright | $2.50 |
| ☐ 41794-0 | **Katie and Those Boys** | Martha Tolles | $2.50 |
| ☐ 40565-9 | **Secret Agents Four** | Donald J. Sobol | $2.50 |
| ☐ 40554-3 | **Sixth Grade Sleepover** | Eve Bunting | $2.50 |
| ☐ 40419-9 | **When the Dolls Woke** | Marjorie Filley Stover | $2.50 |

### BEST SELLING APPLE TITLES

| | | | |
|---|---|---|---|
| ☐ 41042-3 | **The Dollhouse Murders** | Betty Ren Wright | $2.50 |
| ☐ 42319-3 | **The Friendship Pact** | Susan Beth Pfeffer | $2.75 |
| ☐ 40755-4 | **Ghosts Beneath Our Feet** | Betty Ren Wright | $2.50 |
| ☐ 40605-1 | **Help! I'm a Prisoner in the Library** | Eth Clifford | $2.50 |
| ☐ 40724-4 | **Katie's Baby-sitting Job** | Martha Tolles | $2.50 |
| ☐ 40494-6 | **The Little Gymnast** | Sheila Haigh | $2.50 |
| ☐ 40283-8 | **Me and Katie (the Pest)** | Ann M. Martin | $2.50 |
| ☐ 42316-9 | **Nothing's Fair in Fifth Grade** | Barthe DeClements | $2.75 |
| ☐ 40607-8 | **Secrets in the Attic** | Carol Beach York | $2.50 |
| ☐ 40180-7 | **Sixth Grade Can Really Kill You** | Barthe DeClements | $2.50 |
| ☐ 41118-7 | **Tough-Luck Karen** | Johanna Hurwitz | $2.50 |
| ☐ 42326-6 | **Veronica the Show-off** | Nancy K. Robinson | $2.75 |
| ☐ 42374-6 | **Who's Reading Darci's Diary?** | Martha Tolles | $2.75 |

**Available wherever you buy books...or use the coupon below.**

**Scholastic Inc. P.O. Box 7502, 2932 E. McCarty Street, Jefferson City, MO 65102**

Please send me the books I have checked above. I am enclosing $_____
(please add $1.00 to cover shipping and handling). Send check or money order—no cash or C.O.D.'s please.

Name _____

Address _____

City _____ State/Zip _____

Please allow four to six weeks for delivery. Offer good in U.S.A. only. Sorry, mail order not available to residents of Canada. Prices subject to change.                                          **APP 888**